Intermezzo

Business Matters

Wisteria Tearoom Mysteries

Intermezzi (Interludes)

The Intermezzi are not mysteries, nor are they full-length novels. They are interludes, shorter stories about the series characters.

Intermezzo
Business Matters

A Wisteria Tearoom Interlude

Patrice Greenwood

Evennight Books
Cedar Crest, New Mexico

This is a work of fiction. All of the characters, organizations, and events portrayed in this novel are either products of the author's imagination or are used fictitiously.

INTERMEZZO: BUSINESS MATTERS

Copyright © 2022 by Patrice Greenwood

Evennight Books
P.O. Box 1644
Cedar Crest, NM 87008-1644

evennight.com

Cover photo: Pati Nagle

ISBN: 978-1-952653-10-0

First Edition August 2022

for Patricia D.
Remember the rellenos!

Acknowledgments

As ever, my heartfelt thanks to Chris Krohn and to the Treehouse Writers (treehousewriters.com) for their assistance and support.

A Note from the Author

Dear Readers,

This book is a little different. I'd like to explain a few things so you'll know what to expect.

~ This is not a mystery. The next Wisteria Tearoom Mystery is coming soon.

~ This is not a novel. It's a novella, in this case about two-thirds as long as a novel. Okay, it's almost a novel.

~ This is not "leftovers." It is not text that was edited out of a novel. It's all original material that is focused on the characters in the series.

~ Where it fits: this story falls between book 8, *A Valentine for One*, and book 9.

~ Finally, if you have not encountered the Wisteria Tearoom books before, this is not the best one to start with. Any of the mysteries—the full-length novels—is a better choice. Since they're sequential with an over-arching storyline, I recommend starting with book 1, *A Fatal Twist of Lemon*.

I hope you enjoy this little interlude. Meanwhile, I'm off to the writing chair to work on the next book.

—Patrice Greenwood

WARM LIGHT FROM CAFÉ CANDLES glowed along the table, glinting from crystal wine glasses, iced tea glasses, and water goblets—empty, filled, and in between—creating a symphony of light resonant of an evening of enjoyment. Kris scraped a last bit of chocolate from her dessert plate and closed her eyes as she savored it. Santacafé had given us a delightful dinner, and now it was time to get down to business.

Picking up the folder I had rested against the foot of my chair, I took out a handful of pages and passed them to Kris, Julio, my Aunt Nat, and Hanh, whom I had decided to include at the last minute. She was second-in-command in the Wisteria Tearoom's kitchen, and might be the chef someday. I valued her opinions. I also wanted to teach myself to be less intimidated by her.

"Here's my agenda," I said as they looked over the pages. "Feel free to chime in if you have concerns I haven't covered."

I laid the copy I had kept for myself beside my notepad. The list was short, but each item on it would take a while to cover. I hoped we'd be able to finish before the restaurant closed.

I took a sip of water. Julio, seated to my right, gave me a wry look and poured the last of the red wine into my glass, carefully keeping the dregs back in the bottle's shoulder. I nodded my thanks.

"First, then, is staffing. We need a full-time manager for the gift shop. Kris has run the numbers, and we can afford it. Does anyone know someone they'd like to recommend?"

Silence for a moment, then Nat spoke up. "Are you going to offer it to the servers?"

"Well, I thought about it, but most of them are in school or have other reasons for wanting a flexible schedule. This is a full-time job, and I know *you* don't want that."

"Right," Nat said. "What about Dale?"

"I can mention it to him, but I have a feeling he wouldn't be interested."

Of all the servers on my staff, Dale spent the least time in the gift shop. The others were more likely to straighten and restock the merchandise, or acquaint themselves with new items when they came in.

Also, in my heart, I wanted to keep Dale as a server. It was good to have a male on the service team, and he was *really* good with the Bird Woman. The thought of promoting him to run the gift shop went a little against my feminist grain.

To be fair, though, I *should* let them all know about the position.

"I can advertise the job," Kris said, "but that means interviewing and all that."

I nodded. "I'd rather spare us the trouble if I can. Please think about it, and if you have any ideas let me know in the next couple of days." I made a note on my pad to mention the opening to the staff. Maybe one of them would have a suitable friend.

"Do we have any other staffing needs?" I asked, looking at Julio. "Is the kitchen covered?"

He nodded, his dark curls free over his shoulders for once, rather than confined by a chef's cap. They were getting longish, I realized.

"We're good for now," he said. "We'll see how we do when the tourist season gets into full swing."

I turned to Kris. "How about the servers? Any scheduling issues?"

"We're okay, though we might need an extra

when things get busier. February strained us a little."

"Yes," I said.

Valentine's Day—that whole week—had been very busy. If we'd had one server sick out, it would have been a problem. Of course, dealing with (another) murder investigation on the property had not helped.

I took a sip of wine. "Well, let's think about adding one more server. Low-priority, but we can start looking. Next: St. Patrick's Day. No event, but I'm planning to have live music again, like we did for Valentine's."

Julio exchanged a glance with Hanh. "We may need Ramon in the kitchen."

"I wasn't going to ask him," I said. "I'm thinking about harp music, not guitar."

"Owen?" Kris asked.

"Yes. I haven't talked to him yet. It's a Thursday, so we won't have an extra work day this time. And it's not a huge romantic holiday. The music will probably book us up solid for that day, but it won't be as crazy as Valentine's."

"We are fairly well booked for March," Kris said.

"Are we?"

She nodded. "I'd say between half and three-quarters booked."

"Wow. Does that include the dining parlor?"

"A few times. People are getting used to it being open for cream tea, but we do have a couple of big parties. Mrs. Olavssen wants it on St. Patrick's Day."

Of course she did. What would it be? A troupe of leprechauns? Céilí dancers?

I sighed. "Well, we can accommodate them, but I have changes in mind for that room. If there are no more questions about St. Patrick's, we'll move on to that item."

Julio raised a hand. "Do you want the menu to be Irish-themed?"

"For the whole month? No. Maybe a couple of items."

He nodded. "Good. I've got a draft done. We can go over it Monday morning."

I made a note, and checked my calendar. Monday was February 22nd. Julio would have a week to finalize the menu for March.

"Anything else?" I looked around the table.

Nat smiled, ever supportive. Although the tearoom would not have existed without her encouragement, it was my thing, not hers. She made suggestions now and then, but the decisions were up to me.

Hanh looked placid, patient. She was habitually quiet, only speaking up when she thought something really needed adjustment. Her silence was part of what intimidated me, as I sometimes got the feeling it was disapproving. But that could be my imagination.

"All right, then," I said. "On to the dining parlor. I'm going to take the table to my new home, and we need to have a little work done on the fireplace—"

Because I'm going to have a hole dug in the wall.

"—so it's a good time to think about changing it up. We don't get enough big parties to keep it booked up, and the cream tea has been a bit chaotic. I'm thinking of dividing the parlor into alcoves instead."

"Great idea," Kris said. "People have been disappointed about Poppy and Hyacinth being gone. Afternoon tea beats cream tea for profitability."

"Yes, and the cream tea is a little hard to manage," I said. "People want to linger."

"They'll be disappointed if we take away cream tea altogether," Nat said.

"I'm planning to serve it outside, on the *portal,* once the weather is warm enough. They can linger there without being a problem."

"Then we'll definitely need another server," Kris said. "And you might want to get some inexpensive china for outdoors. There's bound to be more breakage, and you don't want to lose your fine china."

"True. Could you price some inexpensive stuff for us?"

"Sure." Kris made a note on her agenda. "You could even use paper out there."

"I'd rather not. I've been toying with offering cream tea to go, though."

Kris's brows rose. "I'll price cups and containers."

"Look for eco-friendly, please. I'd like to avoid single-use plastic."

She nodded. "We can use our current pastry bags and boxes. We'll just need cups and something for the cream and curd—unless you're skipping those."

"No, no! Cream is part of cream tea!"

I looked at my agenda, and underlined the note to hire another server. "We've strayed a little. Let's go back to the dining parlor. Nat, will you help me find furnishings?"

"I'd be delighted. Will it be four alcoves, like the main parlor?"

"I was thinking three. One with the fireplace to itself, one with a view out the French doors, and one facing the lilacs out the north windows."

Kris tilted her head. "Do you have a copy of the floor plan with you?"

"The current one? Yes."

I picked up my folder and extracted the ground floor plan, which I handed across to her.

While she gazed at it, I took another sip of wine and checked the time on my phone. Almost nine.

"Your lilac-viewing alcove would be really long and skinny. How about two smaller ones instead? We do get a lot of parties of two."

"I don't want to have the fireplace shared, though," I said. "It's awkward."

"You don't have to," Kris said. "May I draw on this?"

"Sure."

She marked a couple of lines on the plan and handed it back to me. She had drawn a line vertically at the north edge of the fireplace, and another dividing the room horizontally, resulting in two larger alcoves and two smaller ones.

Nat leaned toward me to look at it. "That looks good! You could bring Hyacinth and Poppy back as the small ones."

"I'm thinking of making Poppy the fireplace one, actually. The northeast one will be Lilac, and the one looking out the French doors will be Marigold."

"Ah—so all the wing chairs will come back into alcoves!"

"Yes. We'll need some additional furnishings, but that will give us a start."

"I like it!"

I sketched in an entryway giving access to the two smaller alcoves, similar to the main parlor, which was divided by heavy drapes hung from the ceiling. We had started with screens, originally, but the fantastic drapery decorations that Kris and her friends had put up for their Halloween masquerade had made me realize we could use drapes to divide the alcoves. They were easier to move around and provided better soundproofing.

Looking at the picture, I drew a dotted line in the main parlor, extending Rose to the north side of the fireplace there and making Iris smaller. Then I did the same in the south parlor, giving Violet the fireplace and making Dahlia smaller.

"What do you think of this?" I asked, showing Nat.

She gave a slow nod. "Yes. It will make the fireplaces easier to tend."

"May I see?" Kris said. Nat handed the page to her. "Oh, that's good! That gives us four smaller seatings."

"Is that too many?" I asked.

"Not at all. Guaranteed, they'll fill up with parties of two or three, and we'll be able to accommodate bigger groups in the enlarged alcoves. Up to eight, it looks like."

She handed the page to Hanh, who looked at it, nodded, and gave it to Julio.

"What about groups larger than eight?" he asked.

"We can open up Marigold and Poppy into one big alcove," Nat said. "We can even add the two smaller ones if we need to. So the dining parlor will still work for large parties."

"That's good," Julio said. "Big groups closest to the kitchen makes it easier to serve them."

I accepted the page back from Julio and looked at it again. "Yes. This will work. We'll have to move the curtains for Rose and Violet."

"Shouldn't be a problem," Kris said, making a note. "We'll be installing new ones in the dining parlor. It can all be done at once."

My weekends would be busy for a while. Well, they would be anyway, because I needed to move. I put the floor plan back in my folder.

"If we're done with the ground floor, I have some changes planned for the upper floor as well. Since I won't be living in my suite, I think I'll move my office into the bedroom. Then Kris can have my current office, and the gift shop manager can have hers."

"Brilliant!" Kris said. "I was going to ask about a desk for the gift shop person."

"If you like, we can leave yours where it is and get you a new one."

"And another file cabinet, please? The one we have is stuffed."

"Okay."

This was starting to feel expensive. I took a

deep breath. Kris would price everything out and let me know if the money would be a strain. We could wait on some things, if need be.

I did want to get the dining parlor changed before April, though. I hadn't put it on the agenda for this meeting, but I wanted to have a special event to celebrate the tearoom's first anniversary. It was time to start planning.

I looked over my notes. "I think that's everything. Any questions?"

Silence for a moment, then Hanh raised her hand.

"Yes, Hanh?"

"I would like to take a day off on May 14."

I checked my calendar. A Saturday. *Not* the day before Mother's Day, fortunately.

"I'm sure that would be fine," I said.

"Thank you." She nodded—or was it a small bow? It reminded me of Owen's formal courtesies.

Now I was curious. Hanh had never asked for time off before. She'd been working at the tearoom since the fall. I glanced at Kris, looking for any reaction, but she seemed impassive.

Maybe Hanh just wanted a vacation day. She had certainly accrued the time by now. But she had asked so far in advance, it must be for something special.

Don't be nosy, Ellen.

We'd just ask Ramon to cover for Hanh that day. I made a note, though scheduling wasn't technically my responsibility. Kris would take care of it.

"Anything else?" I asked, looking around at everyone. Julio shook his head. Kris picked up her wine glass and drank the last bit.

"Then thank you, all," I said. "We'll do this again."

I finished my own wine as the others began to get up. Kris slung a small, black, beaded purse over her shoulder and paused by my chair.

"This was great," she said. "Really helpful."

"I agree. We should have been meeting like this all along." We'd started having monthly staff meetings, but this was the first meeting of just the administrative team. The need for it had become apparent in February, with the Valentine's Day crush.

I gathered my notes as our waiter quietly stepped forward with the black folder containing the check for our meal. I accepted it, then Kris took it out of my hands.

"Deductible," she said. She glanced at the bill, inserted the tearoom's credit card, which we used for purchasing supplies and so on, and gave the folder back to the waiter. "We shouldn't meet here every time, though."

"Oh, no," I said. "But I wanted to thank you

all. You're all essential to the tearoom's success."

Nat smiled as she draped her warm shawl around her shoulders. "See you tomorrow!"

"Yes," I said. She didn't usually come in on Thursdays, but I was treating her to tea, along with Claudia Pearson. My thank you to them both for working on Valentine's weekend.

A tall young man in chef's whites came up to Julio: Andre, his former roommate. After they exchanged greetings, he turned to me.

"I hope you enjoyed the meal."

"Very much," I said. "Thank you, Andre. Everything was wonderful."

He smiled. "Good."

"Have you booked your tea?" Andre had also pitched in to help us at Valentine's, giving up his weekend to do so, and I had given him a gift certificate good for tea for two as a thank-you.

"Yes," he said. "I'm bringing my partner."

A half-glance toward Julio, who had looked away. History there—they had been more than roommates, I suspected, but Julio was now with Owen Hughes. Who happened to be my new landlord. So convoluted. Santa Fe *was* a small town, though.

I smiled at Andre. "Good! We'll look forward to seeing you."

I collected my folder, purse, and wrap, and

said goodnight to Julio, who looked like he meant to linger and chat with Andre. Nat and Hanh had already left. Kris was signing the credit card slip. I waited for her, gazing at the candlelight still dancing among the glasses on the table. It had been a good evening.

I hugged my wrap close against the chill as Kris and I walked out to the parking lot together. "How often should we meet?" I said, half-musing. "Monthly? Quarterly?"

"Eight times a year," Kris said with a small laugh.

"Okay." Whatever the joke was, she didn't elaborate. "See you tomorrow," I added.

We'd meet as the need came up, I decided, getting into my car.

I dressed for tea right away the next morning, since Nat and Claudia were coming at eleven and I expected to be busy until then. I carried Minuit, my adopted kitten, to her playpen in my office at arm's length, as the dress I had chosen was both lace (vulnerable to snags from tiny claws) and white (magnetic to black fur). She meeped a little as I zipped her in, but took her disappointment out on her ring toy, attacking it with rattling gusto.

I poured myself a cup of tea from the pot atop the wisteria samovar, which I had brewed before getting dressed. Kris was at her desk and glanced up at me.

"Tea?" I offered.

"I've got some, thanks. Let me know when you have a minute."

"I'll check my messages first if that's okay."

"Sure."

Settling at my desk, I took a swallow of Assam. Malty, strong, and bracing. Just what I needed.

A handful of lavender messages slips left over from the previous day sat in my in box, silently tut-tutting. I glanced through them, tossed a couple (sales reps), and started a "call" list with the others. I added Owen to that list, and Phillips, with whom I needed to schedule the extraction from the dining parlor wall of what I hoped was the pistol ball that had killed Captain Dusenberry. And Manny's friend Louie Cordova, whom I would need to repair the damage from that exercise.

My cell phone rang. I picked it up, and sighed. It was my bestie Gina, and I knew what she was going to say.

"Hi, Gina," I said brightly.

"Have you chosen a wedding venue?"

"Not yet."

"Dude, you gotta get it done."

"I know." I picked up a pen and started doodling on one of the message slips.

"If you don't book it soon you'll be getting married at the tearoom," she warned. An option I had already decided against. "Did you see the list I sent you?" she added.

"Yes. I want to go up and check out Hyde Park Lodge."

"You won't like it. There's no kitchen."

I grimaced. "I'd still like to see it. I really want outdoors."

"I know, I know. Go this weekend, okay?"

"I'm moving this weekend."

"So take a break. Go up there with Tony."

Not a bad idea. Tony should have a say in where we'd be getting married. But there was so much to do....

"I'll think about it."

"All right. Let's have lunch and talk about the reception."

"Yes, but not today. I'm booked."

"Tomorrow?"

"Fridays are busy. How about Monday or Tuesday?"

"Tuesday. A lot of places are closed Mondays."

Including my tearoom. I had stuck to closing Sundays and Mondays, with exceptions for holidays that fell on those dates, despite pressure from our customers to open. My staff needed a weekend. *I* needed a weekend.

"Tuesday it is," I said, opening my calendar. "You choose the restaurant."

"Have you been to Piccolino?"

"Yes, Tony took me there. What time?"

"Meet you there at eleven."

"Okay," I added it to my calendar. "See you then."

"Ciao!"

I put down my phone with a sigh. I loved Gina dearly, but she sometimes drove me crazy. Making her my maid of honor might have been a mistake, though she'd have been terribly hurt if I hadn't. And really, she was the obvious choice.

Closing my calendar, I set aside Gina and the wedding plans. I had work to do.

I swallowed the last of my lukewarm tea and got up to pour myself a fresh cup, adding a dollop of milk. Through the doorway of her office I saw Kris watching me. Smiling, I carried my tea in and sat in her guest chair.

"I've priced out a new desk and file cabinet," she said, swiveling her flatscreen monitor so I could see the desk displayed on it. It was sort of Arts-and-Crafts-looking, and very black. I would have chosen something lighter, but it would be Kris's desk. As long as she didn't drape the entire room in black, I was willing to let her follow her taste.

She told me the price, and I nodded. It wasn't cheap, but it wasn't crazy expensive, and quality was worth paying for. She brought up a file cabinet—also black—and horizontal.

"It costs a little more than an upright, but it will fit under the roof behind the desk and take up less space," Kris said.

I nodded. "That works. What about a printer stand?"

"There's one with the set, if you don't mind."

"I don't." Better to get it all at once.

She went on to show me packaging options for the curd and cream to go. I chose round white paper containers over the less expensive plastic. They looked nicer and were better for the environment.

"I'll order a small quantity to start with, and we'll see how they do," she said. "Now, have a look at this."

She brought up an image of tapestry fabric woven with clusters of wisteria blossoms. I gave a little crow of delight.

"Where did you find that?"

"It's new, from the company that did our drapes for the alcoves. Want it for the new ones?

"I want it for the whole tearoom!" The current drapes were solid-colored, a deep violet.

"That might be pricey," Kris said. "I'll see if they'll give us a bulk discount."

"Well, we'll have to get new drapes for Violet and Rose anyway, since the sizes are changing."

"True," Kris said. "They're coming in to measure for all of that on Monday. I can talk to them then."

"Thank you, Kris! What a wonderful find!"

She tapped her keyboard, bringing up a picture of a plain white teacup and saucer. "For outdoor service. There's this, and then this." She changed to another style, very modern-looking. "The second one is slightly less expensive."

I shook my head. "Too stark. I like the first one."

"Okay. When do you plan to start serving the cream tea outdoors?"

"Um. Well, after the anniversary, I think."

"So we don't need to order this right away. I'll do it next month."

"Thanks, Kris. How is all this affecting the budget?"

"Well, the big items will be the new drapes, furniture, and the new staff. We'll know about the drapes after Monday."

The gift shop manager would be expensive. I planned to offer what had been Kris's starting salary. The server, whenever we added one, would get the same as the others—a decent hourly wage. When the tearoom had opened I'd made that our policy, and informed our customers that our prices included compensation to the staff, so that tipping was unnecessary. Several other restaurants in town had done the same, and I supported moving away from a tip economy.

"Can we afford to give the servers a raise on the tearoom's anniversary? At least Dee and Iz, they'll have been here a year. Oh, and Mick, too."

"Maybe a small raise. What about Julio?"

"Yes. He should definitely get a raise."

"I'll run some numbers."

"Thanks."

She turned her screen back, typing notes. "You already gave me a raise, so I don't need another."

"Oh, Kris. You're indispensable, though!"

A small smile curved her lips. "You pay me enough."

"Well, I'd like to give a gift to all the staff for the anniversary. A free tea for two?"

"Maybe for one. I'll cost it out for you."

"Okay. Anything else?"

"That's it for now."

I finished my tea and stood. "Thank you."

She nodded, already absorbed in calculations. I left her to it and returned to my office. Minuit chirped at me, and I couldn't resist reaching into her playpen to give her a scritch. I added some kibble to her bowl, then closed the playpen again and went downstairs.

The tearoom was not yet open, but the kitchen was baking for the first seating. The aroma of rose almond scones made my mouth water despite my light breakfast. I looked in and saw Hanh seated at the break table with a mug of green tea before her, sketching in a notebook. Julio wasn't in the room. Loaves of bread and a bowl of cucumbers sat on a work table, waiting to be made into sandwiches.

I walked over to Hanh, smiling. "Good morning. Where's Julio?"

"Went for a walk."

Break time. I glanced down at Hanh's sketch, which was a two-tiered cake with elaborate floral decorations.

"Is that for a wedding?"

Hanh shook her head. "For Buddha's birthday. That why I asked for the day off. I need to make two like this, for the next day."

"Goodness! Well, I'd want a day off for that, too! Is it a big celebration?"

Hanh nodded, picking up her tea mug. "Big holiday. Biggest day of the year for us."

I'd never heard of Buddha's birthday. It must be rather like Christmas, I supposed. Gazing at the sketch, I wondered if the hanging clusters of flowers on the cake would be wisteria.

"Well, that looks absolutely lovely. What kind of cake will it be?"

"Carrot cake. Vegan."

"Ah." Hanh had ordered a vegetarian entree at the dinner meeting, and I'd never seen her eating meat, that I recalled.

"One is for offering," she added. "The other for the feast."

I slid into the seat across from her. "Do you make cakes every year?"

She nodded. "Last three years, yes. Since I finished school."

"I see. Are there many food offerings?"

Hanh raised her dark eyes to meet mine. "Yes. Also flowers and incense. Big ceremony, and speeches. Then everyone bathe the baby Buddha for good luck."

"You bathe the baby Buddha? Is it a real baby?" I asked, thinking of the live nativity displays that were common at Christmas time.

"A statue. We pour tea over." She pantomimed ladling water over an imaginary statuette.

"Ah."

"Then make a wish."

I nodded. "It sounds like a lovely celebration. Thank you for telling me about it."

She smiled shyly, then picked up her mug of tea. I judged it time to leave her to her break. As

I stood, Julio came in, shedding his coat. He hung it on a hook and took down his apron.

"Cold out?" I asked, joining him by the sink as he tied it on.

"Yeah. Windy."

Fires in the fireplaces today, then. Most mornings I would work on them myself if I had time. I loved a nice, cozy fire, and enjoyed building them. Today I'd leave it to the servers, since I was wearing white. Instead I went up to the gift shop to pass the time tidying and re-stocking any merchandise that was low.

There was still an abundance of pink and hearts on the seasonal display table, though the valentine cards had been put away for next year. One lone black heart mug—my nemesis—remained on the table. I just didn't like the design, though a lot of our customers had. I looked in the storage cupboards beneath the table and found half a dozen heart-shaped ceramic boxes. Those would probably sell. Arranging them on the table, I moved the black mug aside to make room for them, then stood back, ap-praising the display.

Time to get some Irish-themed merchandise for March. Extra Irish Breakfast tea, certainly. We had a few select pieces of Belleek shamrock china to sell. That would go in the center of the table. Lace doilies could be in the seasonal display as well. They didn't have to be Irish lace.

This sort of thing would be handled by the new gift shop manager, I realized. Not that I disliked it, but I *did* have plenty of other things to do.

Such as making phone calls. I'd better get that done before eleven.

Heading upstairs, I met Dale in the hall, carrying a sling of firewood to the main parlor. We exchanged good mornings as we passed, and I remembered that I needed to tell the staff about the job opening. Both openings. I'd mention it at the monthly staff meeting, Tuesday morning.

Returning to my desk, I resisted the temptation to pour myself more tea. I'd be having plenty with my guests in a little while. Instead I took out my "to call" list and a notepad and pen.

Phillips, the crime scene technician who worked with Tony and had located the possible pistol ball in the wall, was first on the list. I got voicemail and left a message asking if he could come extract the ball on Sunday.

Next was Louis Cordova, but I'd wait until I'd heard back from Phillips. I called Owen's number and he answered with a languorous "hello."

"Am I calling too early?" I asked.

"No, no. What can I do for you?"

"I'm looking for some live Irish music for the

tearoom for St. Patrick's Day, and wondered if you'd be interested, or know someone else—"

"I'd be delighted!"

"We'll pay you, of course."

"Of course."

And I knew what he'd do with the money. He'd give it to charity.

"And maybe you know a couple of other musicians who'd be interested," I said. "Perhaps a trio?"

"A duo. I know just the person, but he'll need your permission to take off work," Owen said, sounding amused.

2

I BLINKED. Not Ramon. Not Julio. "Dale?"

"Yes, he plays the Irish whistle," Owen said.

"I didn't know!"

"He's also a mean hand on the bodhran."

That was a kind of drum, I believed. "Not too rowdy, please," I said as I wrote Dale's name next to Owen's on my notepad.

"We'll keep it sedate. What time would you want us?"

"Eleven to six, if that's not too much. Three seatings. You can play the same set for each one, and include substantial breaks. We have half an hour between seatings for changeover."

"So, a two-hour set? Or one and a half?"

"One and a half should be plenty. We can have recorded music during your breaks."

"Entirely doable. I'll talk to Dale about rehearsing."

"Thank you!"

"Where will we be playing?"

"In the hall, by the stairs. Where Ramon was for the Masquerade, if you remember?"

"Ah, yes. That will work, I think. I'll come look, and if there's not enough room for the concert harp, I'll bring the large Celtic one."

"Sounds good."

"Do you want amplification?"

"Um, I guess so." Ramon had used a little amp. "Just enough to reach the parlors."

"We could check it the weekend before. Do our final rehearsal in the tearoom, if that works for you."

"Yes, that would be fine. Maybe the Monday before?"

"Okay. I'll go over all the details with Dale. If you'd tell him about the gig, and that he has your blessing?"

"I will. Thanks."

"My pleasure."

I said goodbye and checked the call off on my list, thinking that pleasure was a word I very much associated with Owen. He was deeply interested in pleasure.

Well, in a way, so was I. The tearoom was designed for it—it was our signature. We worked hard to give our customers enjoyment through the furnishings, the ambiance, the tea, and the service.

Next on the list was Mr. Hidalgo. I wrote "wait" by his name, because I wanted to know the condition of the pistol ball—or if it even *was* a pistol ball—before talking to him.

The next couple of calls were business-related. I dealt with them, crossed them off, and decided I had earned my reward: some of that Wisteria Tearoom signature pleasure with Nat and Claudia.

The kitten was napping. I checked that she had everything she needed, then looked in on Kris. "I'm heading downstairs for my tea. Need anything?"

"No, I'm good. Thanks."

"See you in a couple of hours."

A murmur of voices rose to meet me as I came down the stairs. It was almost eleven, and early arrivals were waiting in the hall or browsing the gift shop. I glanced into the butler's pantry—very busy with the servers brewing tea —then went up to the shop.

My arrival created a bit of a stir, as several of the waiting guests were regulars and wanted to say hello. I greeted them all and drifted closer to the fireplace, which was back-to-back with the one shared by Dahlia and Violet. The fire's warmth was delightful, and I stood chatting there until Nat and Claudia came in, both looking splendid.

Claudia was the picture of silvery grace in a gray linen skirt and jacket over a white silk blouse, with a little matching gray pillbox hat and white gloves. Nat wore her (second) wedding dress, a red velvet ensemble in traditional Navajo style, with a classic silver-and-turquoise squash blossom necklace. She and I had made that dress together in her living room, along with my matching blue one, which would have been a more sensible choice than lace this morning, I reflected. Ah, well.

I greeted Claudia and Nat with hugs and led them back to Dahlia, exchanging a glance with Dee who stood at the hostess stand waiting to take guests to their alcoves. She smiled and nodded as the mantel clock in the main parlor chimed the hour, a sound I could just make out through the chatter.

The fire flickered softly, partly hidden by the curtain that separated Dahlia from Violet. My mind went to the upcoming changes: Dahlia would no longer share the view of the fireplace. Instead it would be small and cozy, while Violet would be larger with the focus centered on the fireplace and the portrait of Vi above it. Both alcoves would be better for it, though I wanted to come up with something special for Dahlia in place of the fire. Iris, in the main parlor, had a window to compensate, but Dahila had none. I'd have to think about that.

Dee came through leading a party of three young women, chattering as they went, to Violet. They even were more lightly attired than I was—one of them had on a sleeveless dress and sandals—but they were too excited to be here to notice the chill, I supposed. The fire would soon warm them.

Soon after Dee went back out, Iz brought in a pot of tea and poured the first cup for us, then went away again, promising to bring our tray shortly. The gentle aroma of Darjeeling wafted up from my cup, and I inhaled a deep breath before sipping.

"Ah, this is lovely," Claudia said. "I've been wanting this meal ever since I smelled it all day last weekend."

"Well, you earned it!" I said. "Thank you so much for your help."

"It was fun. I'd have done it for free."

"Me, too!" Nat said, picking up her cup.

That was generous of her, I knew. Nat had given up a lot of time to the tearoom lately. More than she wanted to. I paid her, just as I had paid Claudia and Andre, but she didn't really need the money and would no doubt be glad to have more free time once we hired the gift shop manager.

"Well, I wouldn't expect anyone to work for us for free," I said. "We're a business, we can afford to pay our staff."

"True," Claudia said. "Volunteering has its rewards, though. I started as a volunteer at the Trust."

I added a little milk to my tea. "Did you?"

Nat chuckled. "Yes, and then Sylvia wheedled her into joining the staff."

"Sylvia was good at wheedling." Claudia nodded.

"I knew what she was up to," Nat said. "She tried to get me to volunteer too, but I did my time as a candy striper back in the day."

I hadn't heard of that. "Candy striper?"

"Yes, helping in the hospital," Nat said. "I did it when I was a teenager. Now they're just called volunteers, since there are more boys doing it. But we used to wear these candy-striped pinafores. We'd help deliver mail and meals to the patients, or just keep them company when they didn't have visitors."

"I didn't know you did that!"

"It was long ago, when I was in school. Before you were born."

Iz slipped through with a teapot for Violet, where the young ladies were still chattering. I finished my tea and lifted the cozy from our pot, offering a warm-up to the others before filling my cup.

"Claudia," I said, "I know you're busy with the Trust, but now that you've seen how our gift shop runs, do you know of anyone who might like to manage it? We're looking for full-time."

"Hm. No one comes to mind immediately, but I'll think about it."

"Thanks."

Our tea tray arrived, and we busied ourselves with consuming the savories. I went for the *bastilla* first, since they were warm from the oven. A delightful morsel of chicken and almonds, cinnamon and powdered sugar, bundled in crispy filo pastry. Blissfully messy.

"Have you decided which opera you'll be seeing this summer?" Claudia asked me.

"Oh—no, I haven't had time to look at it."

"Better do it soon. The prices are about to go up."

"Thanks for reminding me. It's been, well, busy as you know."

Nat picked up a slice of baguette spread with brie. "What are you planning for the tearoom's anniversary?"

"Oh, I'm just toying with ideas so far—nothing concrete."

"But a party?" Claudia said. "Or just a special menu?"

"I think we'll have an event, yes."

"With music?"

"Yes."

"Manny can connect you with the mariachis," Nat said, with a laughing sidelong glance at me.

"Thanks. I was thinking more string-quartet."

Or maybe harp, but I didn't want to impose on Owen again so soon after St. Patrick's Day. His performance here would amount to volunteering, since he, too, needed no extra income.

I am surrounded by kind and generous people, I reflected. Sipping tea, I dwelt silently on how grateful I was to all of them.

"How are the wedding plans coming?" Nat asked.

"That's right!" Claudia said, turning to me. "Congratulations!"

"Oh, thanks! They're, coming," I said. "Still looking for a venue."

"Not in church?" Claudia asked.

"No, she wants outdoors," Nat said, shooting me another sidelong glance. "You should check with the Opera,"

I gave her a quelling look. "*Much* too big. I'm thinking more like a garden somewhere."

"The new museum has a nice courtyard," Claudia suggested.

New was a relative term; the new building at the New Mexico History Museum had opened several years ago, behind the Palace of the Governors. Another modern intrusion on Captain Dusenberry's former domain, Fort Marcy Post.

"Hm. I hadn't thought of that," I said. "I'll walk over and look at it." I needed to talk to Bennett Cole at the museum anyway, about donating Maria Hidalgo's letters.

"Might be a bit public," Nat said. "But it's worth a look."

"Thanks," I told Claudia, and picked up the pot to refill her cup.

We continued to chat as we worked our way through the scones and sweets and subsequent pots of tea. Our two hours passed swiftly, and before we knew it Iz brought us warm, lavender-scented towels for our hands. Nat took a deep sniff of hers before wiping her fingers.

"Ahh. The perfect lagniappe," she said.

I gave a comfortable sigh as the lavender wafted around me. I was warm, well-fed, and for the moment I'd had enough tea.

"Thank you both for joining me, and for all of your help."

"You know it's our pleasure," Nat said.

Pleasure. I smiled. That was the word of the day.

Having indulged myself, I was determined to be virtuous for the rest of the day. I caught Dale in a spare moment and told him about the music plan. He was delighted. I checked in with Kris, who informed me the drapers were coming the next morning to measure for the new alcove drapes. Then I stationed myself at my desk, where I spent the early afternoon catching up on neglected to-dos that were lower priority. We were finally getting back to normal—sort of—after Valentine's. The tearoom was still busy, but no longer crazy.

Gina texted me a *second* list of potential wedding venues, which guilted me into looking at her first list. Mostly hotels, several of which I'd already considered. None appealed. I looked at her new list, with the same result.

I'd better check out the museum courtyard. It was too late today, and I wasn't dressed for walking. Tomorrow was Friday, bound to be busy, but maybe I could slip away for a break.

The other possibility was Hyde State Park, on the road up to the ski hill and, incidentally, to Ten Thousand Waves. Closer to town that street was called Artist Road—and gave access to the townhome that would be my new home—but the name became Hyde Park Road farther up.

I spent a mental moment luxuriating in a hot tub at 10k Waves. Time to schedule another visit,

I thought, sighing with longing for pine trees, blue skies, and the gentle sound of water. And maybe a hot stone massage.

There was a hot tub at the townhome, though. And Tony was there. I hadn't seen him in a couple of days, because he was having one of those weeks where he was intently involved in an investigation and basically non-verbal about everything else. I sent him a text asking if he'd like to meet for dinner Friday evening. He'd probably say no.

I could just go over to the townhome tonight. Pack an overnight bag, surprise Tony.

Except he didn't love surprises.

Another sigh. What I *really* should do was start packing to move. I felt reluctant to do so, mostly because I didn't like moving. But I had to start preparing, because my uncle Manny was bringing his truck to move my bed and the dining table on Sunday.

I looked up at the sloping ceiling above my desk, and the stained glass ceiling lamp I'd indulged in when I moved in. Quirky old Victorian house. I'd enjoyed living here. I would miss it.

None of which was work.

I blinked, coming back from the rabbit-hole I'd wandered down. Looking at my list, I was about to pick up my desk phone when my cell rang. A hope that it was Tony died when I looked and saw that the caller was Owen.

"Hi, Ellen," he said when I answered. "I'm downstairs. Do you have a minute to come talk?"

"Sure."

Talking with Owen was work, in this case. It was also pleasure, but because it was work I needn't feel guilty about abandoning my less attractive chores and going downstairs.

Owen was standing at the foot of the staircase, in the space where he'd be playing on St. Patrick's Day, and with him was Dale looking natty as always in his work attire: dress shirt and slacks, brocade vest, and bow tie. Today the color palette was muted blues with touches of green in the brocade.

The mantel clock in the main parlor happened to chime as I arrived. I paused, and Owen and Dale both stood still, looking toward the parlor and reminding me strongly of the masquerade, where everything had come to a stop when the clock chimed the hour. Ghosts of fantastical costumes flitted through my memory, including Owen in a jewel-encrusted frock coat and a mask of leaves.

The Westminster chimes concluded, and the clock struck the hour: three o'clock. The second seating had half an hour to go. With guests taken care of, Dale had a little time to spare.

"Hi, Ellen," Owen said, turning toward me as

the sound of the clock faded. He was wearing his black wool coat over a gray turtleneck and black jeans, long hair caught back with a silver sandcast clip. All the dark clothing was rather stark, but his smile did away with any sense of gloom. "There's enough room for us here, but we're kind of going to block the stairs a bit," he said. "Will there be a lot of traffic on them?"

"Not usually. Kris and I may come and go."

"I can be on this side," Dale said, stepping to the foot of the staircase. "I'll need something to hold my instruments, but it can be against the wall and I'll stand, so I can step out of the way if I need to."

Owen moved in line with the banister and a couple of paces to the west. "Then the harp will be here."

"Is there enough room for the concert harp?" I asked.

"Yes, the biggest issue is front-to-back space, because I have to lean it back to play, and there's plenty of room that way." He gestured toward the south wall. It looked like he and Dale might be a little cozy, but they wouldn't completely block the stairs, and they'd be out of the traffic in the hallway.

"I wanted to check now because the musical arrangements differ between the concert harp and the Celtic," Owen said. "I need to know which way to rehearse."

"Well, I suppose the Celtic harp would be perfectly appropriate," I said.

"True, but the concert harp is more versatile. And the sound will carry farther."

"Ah. Then that's better."

"Speaking of which, the room that will get the least sound acoustically is the dining parlor," Owen said, taking a couple of steps in that direction and gesturing. "Would it be all right to place a speaker about here?"

He was standing roughly midway along the side of the staircase.

I bit my lip. "I'm concerned about cables being a trip hazard."

"It would be a Bluetooth speaker. Cordless."

"Oh. I suppose that would be all right, as long as no one kicks it by mistake."

"Better to tuck it at the back of the stairs," Dale said, moving there and indicating where he meant, the dead space behind the staircase. "The servers come and go along the hall, but if it's here it will be out of the way."

"That should work," I said.

Owen nodded. "Good call." He turned to me. "Do you have time to go over some music? I've got a preliminary list."

"All right," I said. "Let's go upstairs."

"Can Dale join us?"

Iz emerged from the butler's pantry, carrying the chimes we used to warn guests that their teatime was coming to an end. She stepped into the main parlor and began playing them.

"I'd better check on my alcoves," Dale said. "I can come up in a few minutes, when they're gone."

"That's fine," I said. "Bring some scones. I'll make tea in the meantime."

He grinned. "Yes, ma'am!"

As Owen and I started up the stairs, I smiled. Spur-of-the moment cream tea, an easy way to pamper my guest. The kitchen always made a few extra scones.

Not that I needed more scones today, but *one* more wouldn't hurt me.

Maybe I should walk over to the museum after all. Or jog.

I led Owen to the seating area by the front window. "Please make yourself comfortable. I'll make us some tea and be right back."

"Thanks," he said, taking off his coat.

"Let me hang that up for you."

The coat rack was by the top of the stairs. I put Owen's coat on a hook, then stepped to the samovar to check that it had enough hot water to brew another pot. It did, so I went across to my suite and put some oolong into my larger teapot, filled it from the samovar and left it steeping while I set up a tray. I chose three teacups from my small personal collection of absolute favorites: wisteria for me, green leaves for Owen, malachite and gold art deco for Dale. To these I added small plates for the scones, milk and sugar, silverware, lace-edged napkins (serviettes, the British called them, as "napkin" had an unfortunate different meaning in the U.K.).

I loved tea things. The array of pretty china made me smile. I dropped a cozy over the teapot and added it to the tray along with the timer, then carried everything out to the window area, where Owen had made himself comfortable in an armchair.

"Wow, I wasn't expecting a feast," he said as I set the tray on the low table.

"It's just cream tea."

"It's not 'just' anything. This is elaborate!"

"Well, elaborate is what I do, I suppose."

He gave a delighted smile. "And that is why I admire you."

I checked the timer—tea almost ready—and kept it in my hand so I could turn it off quickly.

"When will you be joining Tony?" Owen asked. He meant when would I be moving in.

"This weekend we're moving my bed and the dining table. And the cat."

"Ah. The essentials. Whither the cat goes, is home."

I chuckled.

"Wait, do you mean the dining table down-stairs?" he asked. "In the Captain's room?"

"Yes. It was my mother's. We're making some changes to the parlor."

"I am all anticipation!"

The timer began to chirp. I shut it off and removed the infuser from the teapot.

This weekend would be nuts. Not only were we moving the big pieces *out*, and (I hoped) extracting the pistol ball from the wall, but I had to move furniture *in* to the dining parlor, to accommodate the few reservations we had for it until the changeover to alcoves was complete.

Dale arrived carrying a plate of scones, curd, and cream. He settled beside me on the sofa, putting the scones on the table. The complex aroma of oolong arose as I poured the tea and handed cups to Owen and Dale.

Owen closed his eyes and inhaled the fragrant steam. "Ahh. Lovely. What is this?"

"Iron Goddess of Mercy," Dale said, smiling. "My fave."

"Indeed? That would be Kwan Yin."

"Yes," I said. "It's also called Ti Kwan Yin." I took a sip, pausing first to appreciate the aroma as Owen had done.

"Bodhisattva of Compassion," Owen added.

I glanced at him and found him watching me

with a small smile. Setting down my cup, I offered him the scones, then passed them to Dale.

"Thanks, Ellen," Dale said, putting a scone on his plate along with dollops of curd and cream. "I forgot to bring lunch."

"Did the kitchen not make lunch today?"

"They did, but it was soup, and I didn't have a lot."

"Take another, then."

He grinned and did so. I took a scone myself, pulled it apart, decorated one half with a dab of lemon curd, and looked out of the window as I savored a bite. Clouds were gathering out beyond the rooftops. Not enough for a storm, I judged, but they would make a pretty sunset.

For a few minutes we enjoyed our tea and scones in companionable silence. When Owen took the last sip from his cup, I picked up the teapot and filled it again.

"Thank you," he said. "This tea is exquisite. Would it be sacrilege to add milk and sugar?"

"Not at all. It's your cup, do as you wish!"

He did so, then sat back comfortably, stirring with his small, silver spoon. I filled my own cup and topped up Dale's, surreptitiously watching Owen enjoying his tea. He closed his eyes again, smiling.

"Bliss," he said, setting down the cup. "Now, let me tell you what I've got so far." He took out his phone and brought up a list. "We should begin with 'Brian Boru's March,' I think. Get the Irish rolling."

"Bodhran?" Dale asked.

"Flute, I think," Owen said, glancing at me. "Maybe a little bodhran at the end."

"Tearoom," I said, looking at Dale. "Peaceful."

Dale gave a mischievous grin, then nodded. "Yes, Mistress."

Owen read off his list, explaining any titles I didn't recognize, singing a few bars now and then. When Dale joined in with him, adding a lilting harmony to a traditional air I didn't know, Kris came out of her office.

"Rehearsing already?"

"Just choosing the music," Owen said.

"Would you like some cream tea?" I asked, not wanting her to feel excluded.

Kris smiled. "Sure. I'll get my cup."

She fetched her favorite black corset cup and saucer from her office, and sat in the chair next to Dale, across from Owen. I supplied her with tea and gave her the plate bearing the last scone, then returned my attention to Owen. His knowledge of Irish music was clearly deeper than mine. The list he'd drafted ranged from Turloch O'Carolan to Enya, and from folk to classical. It would be a lovely set.

"And that's what I've got so far," he said, putting down his phone and picking up his teacup. "I think it's about thirty-five, forty minutes."

"I notice the absence of 'Danny Boy,'" I remarked.

Owen grimaced. "If you insist."

"I don't, but you might get requests for it."

"We can do it at the end," Dale said. "That'll leave them sighing."

Kris laughed.

"No," Owen said, "because the final song must be 'The Parting Glass'. But very well, we'll include Danny."

"Would you sing it?" I asked tentatively.

"I'd rather not."

"I will," Dale said, then looked at Owen. "If that's okay."

Owen quirked an eyebrow. "We'll try it out. "

"Should we charge extra that day?" Kris asked. "For the music?"

I looked at her. "Do we have any bookings?"

"We do, and I'll grandfather those at the regular price if you want. But the minute word gets out about the music, guarantee you we'll sell out."

I sipped my tea, thinking. Would it be greedy to raise the price? I hadn't planned to, but we *had* charged extra for Valentine's Day. And I would be paying Owen, and possibly an extra server since Dale would be making music. And we did have new expenses coming up.

"Maybe Julio can add a special treat to the menu for that day," I said. "Then we could bump the price a little."

Kris nodded. "I'll consult with him."

I uncovered the teapot and lifted the lid. A little tea was left. I divided it between Owen and Dale, since Kris and I had access to the pot on the samovar.

"Thank you for coming, Owen," I said, putting down the pot. "I think it's a lovely set."

"Well, it will be, I hope. At the moment it's a theoretical set. Dale, when would you like to start rehearsing?"

The phone in Kris's office rang while they were sorting out the details. She excused herself and went to answer it, taking her teacup with her. I gathered the teapot and small plates onto the tray, adding my wisteria teacup.

Dale swallowed the last of his tea and handed me his cup. "Thanks, Ellen. I'd better get back downstairs."

"Yes. Thank you, Dale," I added as he picked up the scones plate and headed for the stairs.

Owen was leaning back in his chair, swirling the last of his tea in the cup, gazing down at it with veiled eyes. I liked the way he took deep interest in his tea. There were times when I drank it without thinking, being distracted or hurried, and that was a pity, I decided. Maybe I'd work on paying better attention to my tea.

"This is going to make St. Patrick's special," I said. "Thank you for being willing to play."

Owen looked up at me. "Thank you for the opportunity. I haven't taken the grand harp out in years."

"Is it difficult to transport?"

"Not really. I have a mattress in the back of the SUV, so all I have to do is pack it up and put it in." He finished his tea and handed me the cup and saucer, which I added to the tray.

"I didn't know you had an SUV," I remarked.

"I keep it at the studio. It's handy for moving big things. Speaking of which, do you need help with your move?"

I shook my head. "My uncle is bringing his truck, so we should be fine, but thank you."

He smiled. "I'll look forward to welcoming you home, then. And now I'd better get out of your way. Thank you for the delightful cream tea."

I saw him to the top of the stairs and handed him his coat, then said goodbye and stepped into my office to check for new messages. Nothing urgent, and Kris was still on the phone. I fetched the tea tray and took it to my suite, where I washed up the china and silver. When everything was put away, I returned to my desk and started a to-do list for the next day.

Drapers to measure: I should be available to discuss the new placements with them. They were coming at nine, before we opened.

Furniture for the dining parlor: Nat and I were going shopping in the afternoon, starting with antique and consignment places. Not the best timing since Friday would be busy, but it had to be done. We needed to set up the new alcoves for next week.

On a separate slip of paper, I started a list of what to look for. We had the chairs and tables from Hyacinth and Poppy, and the original chairs from Marigold-that-was, but we'd need two more chairs and two low tables to provide enough seating for eight.

I could use the wing chairs from my suite, I supposed, but at least one of those would be going to the townhome, eventually. They were my comfort chairs, upholstered in dark green velvet. I could curl up in one and pretend I was in a mossy forest nook.

Until the new drapes were done, we'd need dividers for the new alcoves. Fortunately, I'd kept all the screens from the main parlor when we switched to the drapes. They were out in the shed, and the Poppy and Hyacinth screens were here upstairs.

I glanced toward the hall, thinking about the Hyacinth screen, which I'd placed to divide the front seating area from the rest of the hall. I liked having that separation; maybe I'd keep it. Or I could bring one of the other screens up from the shed. The Hyacinth screen—a floral tapestry of blue and purple and green—went perfectly with the soft blue Hyacinth chairs and really established the garden mood of that alcove, plus it would no doubt please our regulars to see it again. I'd probably keep it there even after the new drapes went in, unless it clashed with the wisteria fabric.

I got up and stepped into Kris's office. "Can you show me that fabric for the drapes again?"

"Sure," she said, and brought it up with a few keystrokes. "They agreed to give us a discount for a bulk order, by the way. And they'll quote it both ways—just the new drapes, and the whole tearoom."

"Wonderful!" I gazed at her monitor, trying to fix the image in my head, then stepped to the doorway to look out at the Hyacinth screen. The two together *might* be too busy. "Can they bring a sample of the fabric tomorrow?" I asked.

"They're going to," Kris said.

"Perfect. Thanks."

Returning to my desk, I glanced at my list

and added *look at museum courtyard* to the bottom. I probably wouldn't get to that one on Friday. Sorry, Gina.

It was almost five-thirty. Downstairs, the final seating would be winding down. I decided to get a little exercise and go down to check on the tearoom.

Two women and a young girl were in the hallway, putting on their coats. I slipped past them with a smile and a nod, and headed to the gift shop. A vision in bright pink and purple brought me up short in the doorway: the Bird Woman, standing by the seasonal table and holding the last of the black heart mugs. Her dress was hot pink with bell sleeves, and her hat was a matching pink with an explosion of purple feathers coming out of the top, looking rather like a giant, upside-down fuchsia blossom. Her purple gloves and the wide sleeves made it look like her arms ended in two more blossoms.

"Hiya, Ellen," she called, catching sight of me. "When are you going to put out your Irish stuff?"

"Oh—ah, probably on the first?"

"Got any pots of gold? I need a dozen."

"Pots of gold? I don't think so."

"Eh, I'll get 'em at the craft store, I guess. Wanted to ask you first, though."

"That's kind of you," I said.

"When's the wedding? I don't want to miss it," she said. "My calendar gets filled up fast."

Oh dear. She was expecting to be invited.

"In September," I said, somewhat evasively. "We haven't booked a venue yet."

"Better get on it. All the hotels go fast."

"We'll have it outdoors, I think. I haven't found the right place yet."

"Outdoors?"

"Yes, I'm looking for a place with a garden. Or maybe a park."

I was babbling, I realized. I stepped up to the table and rearranged the heart boxes, seeking equilibrium. The Bird Woman still flustered me. She was kind and generous to a fault, but her behavior was—unpredictable. That continued to knock me off balance.

I glanced up at her, since she was un-characteristically silent. She was gazing at me thoughtfully.

"I'll see what I can do," she said, nodding.

"Oh, you don't have to—"

"Got any more of these left?" She held up the mug.

"That's the last one," I said.

"I'll take it."

She stepped to the counter and handed the mug to Dale, who was standing there. He shot me a glance, and got out a sheet of lavender tissue to wrap it in.

I took a deep breath, managed a smile, and withdrew. Heading back to the kitchen, I found Mick there alone, washing china. Julio and Hanh had gone home.

I stood in the center of the room between the work tables, deliberately taking slow, deep breaths. The Bird Woman would not bring chaos to my wedding. I could fend off any well-meaning attempts to help. A vision of a wedding in the middle of a theme park flashed through my mind, with dancing animal-costumed people and a mariachi band. I swiftly banished it.

This was *my* wedding, or rather Tony's and mine, and no one else would make it into something we didn't want. Not the Bird Woman, not Gina. No one.

Tony's voice was missing from the plans, come to think of it. Maybe he wasn't interested, but I ought to discuss it with him. Past tradition made the wedding the responsibility of the bride's family, but I wanted us to step into marriage as equal partners. I wanted it to be Tony's wedding as much as mine.

He had commented that he'd just as soon go to a Justice of the Peace, which implied that he didn't care about ceremony and tradition. He was willing to go with whatever I wanted, but since he would be in the middle of it, I wanted to make sure he was comfortable—as comfortable as he *could* be. I suspected his cop-self would be on guard in the midst of a gathering. It wouldn't be huge, but we had family and friends to include, and the guest list would probably approach a hundred people.

Invitations. Oh, argh. We needed to finish the guest list. I really had to talk with Tony, as soon as he had the time.

A small clink of china roused me, and I realized I was staring out the window. Dusk was falling outside. I suddenly wanted to curl up with a book by a fire, but I had too much to do.

Turning, I saw Mick dancing to music I couldn't hear. He paused to place a clean cup carefully in the rack. That gentle, mindful movement calmed me. Leaving him to his work, I went upstairs.

Kris was on her way out, and we traded farewells at the top of the stairs. I went into my office. Minuit began to cry for her supper, and I gave her a treat to appease her while I tidied my desk and shut down my computer.

The few new messages could all wait. No response to my text from Tony. Disappointed, I knew it meant that he was focused on his work and wouldn't relish interruption.

Collecting Minuit from her playpen, I hugged her for comfort as I went across to my suite. I fed her, then changed into comfortable (warmer) clothes and made myself a virtuous salad for dinner. As I ate it at the small café table, I looked around the suite, remembering all the work I'd done setting it up: painting, choosing furniture and decorations, creating a "fireplace" of candles beside the brick wall of the chimney. The first time we'd made fires downstairs, the candles had all melted because I'd put them too close to the chimney.

Three more nights here. I needed to get to work.

After cleaning up my dishes I went into my bedroom, put my big suitcase on my bed, and opened my wardrobe to choose clothes for the next week. It meant thinking about what I'd be wearing to work all week, and what I wanted to wear at home.

Home. The meaning of the word was changing. This suite would still be my space, but it would no longer be my home. My desk would go in here where the bed was, and I'd be leaving the stained glass ceiling lamp in my old office for Kris, who would love it, I was sure.

Maybe I'd get a new stained glass lamp for in here? There was no ceiling fixture in this room. I'd have to get an electrician in to wire it up.

That could wait. There were a hundred more urgent tasks to be done. I pulled out my dresses for the week and turned to put them in the suitcase.

Minuit was sitting in it, watching me with curious eyes.

"No, darling. You're going on Sunday."

I reached for her, but she hopped out of the case, evading my grasp. I folded the dresses into it and closed the lid to prevent her nesting in them, then went to my dresser for stockings, undergarments, and casual clothes.

When the suitcase was full, I set it by the door and took stock of what remained in the wardrobe and my dresser. The wardrobe was staying, since I had a huge closet at the town-home and wanted the storage space here, as well as the anchor of a familiar piece of furniture in its familiar place.

A long, flat, white box sat on the topmost shelf. I took it out, set it on the bed, and opened it. Soft silk and lace nestled in a bed of tissue paper. My wedding dress.

There were a million things to do before I would put this dress on and exchange vows with Tony. The wedding seemed far away, and also seemed to be approaching rather fast.

We'd get there. Smiling softly, I folded the tissue back over the dress and closed the box.

Manny's truck was big enough for the bed and dresser as well as the dining table and chairs,

I was pretty sure. Taking the bedroom furniture now would mean I probably wouldn't have to bother him again.

I checked the time. Not quite eight. Plenty of time for more packing.

Music would help. Sorting through my old CDs, I put on a Clancy Brothers and Tommy Makum album that my father had given me when I was a teen, no doubt hoping to expand my musical horizons. I had liked it, and had all the songs memorized, but I hadn't bothered to get more of their albums.

I fetched empty boxes from the storeroom behind Kris's desk, took them back to my bedroom, and started filling them, dancing and sometimes singing along with the music. A couple of the songs were on Owen's playlist for St. Patrick's Day, including "The Parting Glass," which came up just as I finished filling a box with shoes. I paused to appreciate the music.

A quiet song; a song of farewell. My heart welled with emotion as I listened. I sang softly along with the end of the final verse:

> *But since it falls unto my lot*
>
> *That I should rise and you should not,*
>
> *I'll gently rise and softly call*
>
> *Good night and joy be with you all.*

Minuit hopped onto the bed and mewed. I put the shoes with the other boxes by the door and picked her up for a cuddle.

Now it felt real. I was moving. New home, new adventure. New life.

With Tony.

I checked my cell, but he hadn't answered. It was not yet nine. If I took the suitcase and boxes over to the townhome, I wouldn't be waking him up, and maybe I'd get a chance to see him.

Yes.

I gave Minuit some treats to distract her while I shifted things out into the hall, then collected coat, purse, keys and phone, and the box with my wedding dress. Locking Minuit in, I carried the dress down to my car, then fetched the suitcase and the other boxes. The tearoom was silent except for the little creaks of old wooden floors. I locked up and drove to the townhome.

The front porch light was on, crescent moon gleaming cheerfully, but Tony's bike was not there. I used the garage door opener Owen had provided and parked in the one-car garage, closing the door before unloading the boxes.

The house was dark. I set the first box on the kitchen counter and turned on the light.

It looked lived in. The kitchen wasn't *dirty,* but there was a cereal box on the counter and a small stack of unopened mail on the table. Also, two glasses in the sink.

I went over to look at them. They were the glasses we'd been using for whiskey. Manhattans, Mom had called them—I'd unearthed them from the storage shed, and they reminded me of my parents sipping drinks together by the fire. Quality glass, with a slight taper and a massive base for stability.

I opened the cupboard where Tony had put the whiskey and checked the bottle: almost empty. Either he'd been drinking a lot, or he'd had company.

To be fair, I'd helped him drink some of it. I was tempted to have some now. It was good whiskey, a welcoming gift from Owen.

Shaking my head, I fetched my box and carried it to the master bedroom, turning on lights as I went. Tony had already yielded the larger of the two closets to me, so I stacked the boxes inside it, then found my hangars and unpacked the suitcase so my clothes for next week wouldn't get wrinkled.

I checked my phone. Almost ten. Still no Tony, and no text.

Bother.

The hot tub was calling me, but that would make me pretty late and I ought to get a good night's sleep. Tomorrow would be busy. With a regretful glance toward the French doors, beyond which Santa Fe lay glittering, I turned out the lights and headed back to the tearoom.

3

I WAS IN A HOSPITAL, wearing a candy-striped pinafore and bringing cream tea to patients who had no one to visit them. Irish music was playing over the intercom system, and I had to talk one patient out of getting up to dance. When everyone on the floor had their tea and scones, I rolled my tea trolly back toward the kitchen. I had to pass through the nursery, where I stopped to admire Baby Jesus and Baby Buddha, peacefully slumbering in neighboring cribs, both surrounded with halos of glowing light.

My alarm brought me out of it and I startled up, blinking.

That was weird.

Minuit stirred on the other pillow. I stroked her head and got up carefully so as not to disturb her. Didn't work; she jumped down with a thump and a little mew, and ran out to the kitchenette, where her bowl was.

I opened the wardrobe and was momentarily stunned by the absence of most of my clothes. Taking down the dress I had chosen for the day, I carried it to the bathroom, put a little kibble in Minuit's bowl, and took a steamy shower.

Breakfast: oatmeal and a tangerine. I fired up the samovar, made tea, then moved Minuit to her playpen and carried a cup of tea to my desk. No new texts or email. I could smell cookies baking downstairs, and resolutely remained in my office. Kris came in and we chatted briefly before she went into her office.

"I nabbed some boxes for moving," I told her.

"Great. We always have plenty."

"Any plans for the weekend?"

"Going to a movie with Cherie."

"How is she doing?"

"So-so. We're making sure she sees someone at least a couple of times a week."

"That's really kind of you, Kris."

She shrugged. Kris didn't like to be fussed over, but it *was* kind, extremely kind, of her to comfort one of Gabriel's previous lovers. Kris might be considered the primary bereaved, but she'd handled Gabriel's death far better than Cherie had.

My cell rang: Gina. Kris left and I answered, carrying my teacup to the samovar to refill it.

"Shall we ask the bridesmaids to join us for lunch on Tuesday?" Gina asked.

"Well, I'd have to check if they're available. Any particular reason?"

"We need to plan the favors and table decorations for the reception. I thought you'd like their input."

"Oh. Sure, why not?"

"Let me know what they say. Have you chosen the venue?"

"I'm going to go look at a couple of places this weekend," I said optimistically.

"Great. Hope one of them is perfect."

Yeah. Me too.

I put down the phone and went into Kris's office. "Gina wants to know if you and Angela would like to join us for lunch on Tuesday. She wants to do planning for the reception."

"You don't need me for that, do you?"

"It's more that your ideas are welcome."

"I'll pass, if you don't mind. Got a lot to do. I'll stay here and mind the fort while you go."

"All right."

I texted Gina with Kris's answer, then texted Angela inviting her to join us if she could. I wasn't sure what her work/school schedule was like, but between them and helping her mother and grandmother, she was usually fairly busy.

At quarter to nine I went downstairs to be available to talk with the drapers. Since I had a few extra minutes, I checked on the gift shop and found Dee filling the pastry case with scones and cookies. Their aroma enticed me; I resisted and headed back to the dining parlor.

Standing by the fireplace, I envisioned the new alcoves. Poppy (fireplace) and Marigold (French doors) would be spacious and comfortable. Lilac and Hyacinth, each with a garden window, would be cozy. I still needed to come up with something special for Dahlia, which would now have no window and no fireplace. A fountain, maybe? Lighted? Windows and fires were sources of lovely light....

My musings were interrupted by the drapers. They had brought me a swatch of the wisteria fabric, which was even prettier in person than on the screen. I told them what I wanted for the parlor, gave them a copy of the floor plan on which I had made notes, showed them Rose and Iris, Dahlia and Violet, and left them to their measuring.

Dee was now restocking bags and pastry boxes in the gift shop. I went to the kitchen to say hello. Julio, Hanh, and Ramon were all busy: Julio was decorating Sachertortes, Hanh was piping macarons, Ramon was making cucumber sandwiches. Temptation everywhere!

I stepped up to the table where Julio was working. The Sachertortes gleamed at me—dark chocolate whispering enticement. I watched in silence while Julio piped "Sacher" on top of one in perfect, tiny, chocolate-on-chocolate script.

"Julio, when you have a minute I'd like to talk about March," I said when he'd finished.

"Aren't we going to discuss the menu on Monday?"

"Yes, and I also have a special request."

"Oh. Okay. After I'm done with these?"

"Sure."

Leaving the kitchen, I escaped the siren call of chocolate and went to the parlors, checking on the floral arrangements and removing a faded bloom here and there. This kept me busy until the drapers were ready to leave. As I saw them out, they promised to send estimates within a day or two.

Now the aroma of baking scones permeated the tearoom. Iz and Rosa were setting up the alcoves for the first seating, passing through the hallway with trays of china, silver and linens. Dale was right, a speaker by the stairs would have been in their way.

Returning upstairs, I held the wisteria fabric swatch up to the Hyacinth screen. They went beautifully together—the fabric was more muted in tone, and the colors harmonized. Hyacinth would be lovely.

Back at my desk, I found texts from both Tony and Angela. Tony said he'd try to find time for dinner and would let me know. Unpromising.

Angela had sent a delighted acceptance to the lunch invitation for Tuesday. I passed the word along to Gina, then browsed the Internet for small, lighted fountains. They were expensive, and none of them seemed perfect for Dahlia. One that I liked, a cascade down shell-shaped cups, was a tabletop fountain and rather small. The outdoor fountains were too big, though. There wouldn't be a lot of room in the new Dahlia.

A photo of a stunning vertical fountain inside a yard-high, narrow tower and with a bowl and tealight on top caught my eye. It was perfect, but when I followed the link, it was no longer available. Nothing else appealed to me. Sighing, I abandoned the search when my phone rang.

"You wanted to ask about March?" Julio said.

"Just if you could add a special treat for St. Patrick's Day. We're having music that day."

"Yes, Owen told me. He's jazzed about it."

"Kris suggested raising the price, and I'd feel better about it if we could add a little something extra to the menu. Just for that day."

"No problem. I'll bring a couple of ideas on Monday."

"Great. Thanks. Did you make lunch today?"

"Just sandwiches. Made more crab salad than we needed yesterday. It's still good but we're making fresh today for the guests."

"Perfect. I'll be right down."

Coat, scarf, purse, keys, shopping list, scritch the kitten. Calling a goodbye to Kris, I headed down to the kitchen and joined Julio at the break table. A plate of sandwiches sat in the middle—crab salad on baguette sections—and I helped myself to one, putting it on a paper plate.

"Thanks. I didn't want to take the time to have lunch at a restaurant."

"Busy afternoon?" Julio asked, picking up a sandwich for himself.

"Nat and I are hunting for furniture for the new alcoves. I'm moving the dining table out on Sunday."

"Oh, wow! Okay, yeah. Let me know if you need help."

"All taken care of, thanks. And you do enough!"

He smiled, then took a bite of his sandwich. I followed suit. On the tea trays the crab salad nestled on a small lettuce leaf in a dainty little cup. As a sandwich it was hearty and delicious. The baguette had been spread with garlic butter and lightly toasted, which was fabulous. I tried to take my time and savor it, though the temptation to gobble was strong.

Just as I ate the last bite, Nat came into the kitchen. "There you are!"

"Mm," I said, and swallowed. "Sorry, I was grabbing lunch. Want some?"

"I ate."

I stood, collected my coat and purse, and tossed my paper plate in a wastebasket. "Thanks, Julio!"

"Happy hunting," he said, as Ramon took my place at the table. Hanh glanced up at me as I passed her. She was filling endive leaves with Waldorf salad. I smiled, and she smiled back slightly.

"Shall I drive?" Nat offered as we went outside.

"Sure. Thanks."

We spent the afternoon crawling Santa Fe's consignment shops and antique stores, where we saw lots of interesting nick-knacks, but few ideal armchairs. There were *no* wing chairs to be had, which made me sad. Apparently they were out of fashion. Also, lilac and lavender were not common colors for furniture at the moment. The closest we found were a couple of chairs upholstered in a roasty plum color, but they were overstuffed and much too large for the cozy alcove we envisioned as Lilac.

Mid-afternoon we found one sweet little

antique wooden chair upholstered with multi-colored floral tapestry. Some of the flowers might be lilacs. Close enough! I had brought the swatch with me, and it looked nice with the chair, so I bought it, but we couldn't take it with us as it wouldn't fit in Nat's car. I promised to retrieve it on Saturday.

At a second-hand store run by a charity we found a lovely cherry coffee table that would be perfect for Poppy. It was larger than the one that had been in the original alcove, which would now do for Lilac. Still no suitable chairs.

As we were hunting through the furniture, a round dinette table—comfortable for four—caught my attention, simply because it was beautiful. The top was made in a sort of star pattern with pie-shaped wedges, a subtle blend of different woods that almost made an ombre. A circle of far too many straight-backed chairs surrounded the table at a distance. Curious. The price tag included the chairs, and the whole set was breathtakingly expensive, perhaps because the woodwork of the table was so especially beautiful. I touched the polished surface, perfectly smooth. If this was a used piece, it had been lovingly cared for.

As I stood admiring it, a tall young man with bushy red hair and glasses, wearing a name badge that said "Rick," joined me. "Want to see how it works?" he offered.

"Works?"

He grinned and reached under the table top. I heard a click, then he spun the top and it expended into a compass star, hidden leaves unfolding from beneath and settling into place to become a table large enough for ten or twelve. Now the chairs encircling it fit perfectly.

"Oh! That's marvelous! Nat, come look at this!"

"It's called a capstan table," Rick said as Nat joined us. He happily collapsed the top and opened it again to demonstrate. I watched the complicated movements of the leaves, marveling at the precision with which they resolved into a smooth table.

I looked at the price again. Now I understood why it was so steep. This table was a work of art.

I also understood why it was here. Not many dining rooms were big enough to accommodate such a wonder. A square room would be best, and that was unusual these days—except in old Victorians like the tearoom. All of my parlors were square.

We could use a conference table, now that the dining table was leaving....

No. The only space for it was upstairs, and the capstan table was *massive*, its pedestal as thick as a young redwood. It would be a nightmare to get up the stairs.

"Thank you for showing us," I said. "It's absolutely lovely!"

Rick smiled and collapsed the table, then reached beneath it again. A locking mechanism, I surmised. One wouldn't want one's dinner to start spinning unexpectedly.

I asked him to ring up the coffee table. He carried it out to Nat's car for us, but it wouldn't fit.

"Darn," I said. "Can I pick it up tomorrow?"

"Sure," Rick said. "I'll put it in the back with your name on it. Just bring your receipt when you come."

Nat caught me stifling a sigh as I got in the car. "Ready for a break?" she asked, and I nodded.

So far the day had been disappointing. There were two more consignment shops on our agenda, but I was getting tired. "Let's grab a cuppa somewhere," I said.

We were at the south end of Cerrillos road. Not a lot of elegant places there—mostly chain restaurants—but I had an idea.

"How about Piccolino? We can share a sweet."

"I don't think I've been there," Nat said.

"It's a nice little Italian place. Locally-owned."

Nat started the engine. "Tell me where to go."

I directed her to the restaurant, which was not far away. Even in the afternoon, it was busy—most of the tables were full, though we didn't have to wait for one. We ordered coffee and shared a slice of almond cheesecake. Homemade, delicious.

"We just need one more chair, right?" Nat asked.

"Yes, and maybe a lamp for Lilac. I'll deal with the other decorations later—I have things in storage."

Mother's things, I was thinking. All her favorite little ornaments were in the storage unit along with the rest of Dad's things. And Mom's china, which I wanted to take to the townhome.

Maybe this year I'd clear out that unit. It would be nice not to pay the rent.

I ate a bite of cheesecake and thought about what was in the storage unit. Much had been disposed of before we'd sold my parents' house. What remained were the things I couldn't bear to part with at the time.

The sleeper sofa from Dad's den was now in the townhome; Tony was sleeping on it until I could bring my bed. Was there a chair that would work for Lilac? I couldn't remember—I hadn't actually spent much time going through all that stuff. In my grief after Dad died, I'd shoved it into storage. The memories were safe there, and couldn't haunt me.

Now, maybe I was ready to let go some more.

There were a couple of metal garden chairs, and a little matching table. Probably too casual for the tearoom, and they wouldn't go with the floral chair we'd found. I might take them to the townhome.

"Penny for your thoughts?" Nat said, picking up her coffee.

"Sorry. Just thinking about moving stuff."

She nodded her understanding. "Such a chore. Would ten o'clock be all right on Sunday?"

"Sure."

"You know, Manny could swing by for the coffee table and that chair before he comes."

"Oh, he's doing enough already! And the place we found the chair may not be open Sunday. Thanks, though. I'm going to ask a friend to help me tomorrow."

Because Owen had kindly offered his SUV. I would text him tonight about getting the chair and the coffee table.

Nat and I finished our coffee and headed out to the last two stores. There were now a few clouds in the sky, and the sun was playing hide-and-seek among them as it headed for the horizon. No suitable chairs at either place, though I did find a pretty stained glass table lamp for Lilac. I bought it, and declared the day's work done.

"Are we going to try again tomorrow?" Nat asked as she drove me back to the tearoom. "We could go to Albuquerque—lots more stores there."

"But harder to bring stuff back. I don't think an armchair would fit in your car."

"True."

"I'll use one of the ones in my suite until we can find another."

Nat turned up the long driveway to the back of the tearoom. "Want to join us for dinner?" she said as she parked.

"I've got a maybe with Tony, but thanks."

"Well, if maybe turns into no, come on over."

Hugs goodbye, and I carried the bag with the lamp in the back door. The tearoom was warm and smelled like cookies. Immediately I relaxed, the day's disappointment shedding from me as I relished the gentle sounds and scents of the final seating. Glancing into the dining parlor, I saw the remains of someone's cream tea abandoned on the table. They had left, and the room was empty, so I stepped in.

Picturing the floral chair and the lamp in the corner that would become Lilac, I smiled. It was coming together.

I wondered how Captain Dusenberry would feel about the changes to his room. Would he care? Would he even notice? Glancing at the chandelier, I saw that it was still.

Hm. I guess we'd find out on Sunday.

⁂

"Of course I can help you! I'd be delighted," Owen said over the phone.

"Thanks. The antique place opens at ten and the charity store at nine," I said, "so if you like we can get the coffee table at around nine-thirty and then go get the chair."

"Pick you up at nine-fifteen, then?"

"Sounds good."

I'd be back at the tearoom before we opened. We could stash the chair and table upstairs until Sunday.

We said goodbye and I glanced at my text messages. I had already read the one from Tony:

> Sorry, babe. Can't do
> dinner. Working late.

Disappointing, but not a surprise. I could take Nat up on her invitation, or I could order a pizza and work on packing some more. There were kitchen things I wanted to take to the townhome, and linens and so on. I should wash the canopy hangings from the bed, since I'd be disassembling them. And there was my office furniture—it would be good to move that on Sunday, while I had help.

Pizza it was.

I called in an order, splurged on delivery, and said goodnight to Kris as I started across the hall to change. She was on her way out with the bank deposit.

"Did you get a chance to look over the ad copy?" she asked, meaning the help-wanted ads for a server and a gift-shop manager that she had put in my in-box. "Should I go ahead and place them?"

"Let's talk about it tomorrow. I'm picking up a couple of pieces of furniture in the morning, but I should be back by ten-thirty."

"Okay. See you then."

As I changed into jeans and a sweater, I thought longingly of the hot tub and Tony. I would reward myself with a soak on Sunday evening, and hopefully Tony would join me. Either way I would see him then, if not before.

I made a salad to go with the pizza, then went downstairs to wait for the delivery. It was just after six, and the tearoom was quiet. Dee was tidying up the butler's pantry, putting away clean china, and her brother was washing up the last round of dishes. The others had all gone home. I made a quick tour of the tearoom, looking for anything that needed doing, but the fireplaces had been tended and the gift shop restocked. In the dining parlor, the remains of the fire radiated gentle leftover warmth. I opened the lace curtains over the French doors so I could watch for the pizza delivery, and sat at the dining table to wait.

This would be Marigold's view. The gold wing chairs would come out of the hall, and sit here with the—oh, blast, I needed another coffee table!

Was there anything of Mom and Dad's that would work? Mom's coffee table was by the front window upstairs, and I used that seating frequently. Maybe I could get another table at the second-hand store? They'd had several—the cherry one was the prettiest, but there might be one that would work for Marigold. I'd look when Owen and I went in the morning.

Headlights approached up the driveway. I met the pizza person—a perky Latina who was probably still in high school—at the door, gave her cash and told her to keep the change, and locked the door before taking the box upstairs.

Dinner alone at my little café table. Well, not quite alone; Minuit was enjoying her own dinner nearby.

After Sunday, I'd be dining in the townhome

(with or without Tony), where I looked forward to having a full kitchen to cook in. Should I even keep the café table here? I might want to have lunch there, sometimes, if the tearoom was busy. The little break table downstairs was only big enough for four, and the staff often had to take turns if they were all having lunch in, such as on bad-weather days. Hm.

Staff. Staff meeting Tuesday morning. Ordinarily we'd use the dining parlor, but now there would be … six chairs available?

Not enough. I really *did* need a conference table, and it would have to go in the upstairs hall. We had some long folding tables in the shed that we used for serving buffet style at events—nothing fancy, but they would do for now. For chairs—well, there were the patio chairs from outdoors, not currently in use.

I foresaw many trips up and down the stairs. My legs would get stronger and I could always use the exercise, I reminded myself. I'd been indulging in a lot of scones, lately.

On that thought, I put away the remaining pizza in my mini fridge, virtuously ate all the salad, and cleaned up my dishes before diving into packing.

The evening passed quickly. Boxing up the spare bed linens and towels and most of the kitchen things took longer than I expected. I kept a few towels and some bare-bones cooking tools —enough to reheat a lunch or serve a cream tea to guests—but the rest went into boxes until there were no more empty ones in the storeroom. Holding the last box, which was rather too small to be practical for much but just big enough for some teacups and saucers, I stood in front of my china shelf, debating on which four teacups to take with me.

These were my very favorite cups and saucers. Each set had fond memories associated: the sweet little cup with pink roses that Mom had bought me as a souvenir of our trip to England (my very first teacup), the breathtaking blue and gold French style cabinet cup, a Paragon cup adorned with sweet violets, a classic chintz....

It shouldn't be a tough decision. I wasn't getting *rid* of any of them. I just needed four cups for serving tea at home, to myself and Tony and a couple of guests.

The French cup, I decided. I took it down, carefully wrapped it and its saucer in tissue, and put them in the box. The violets. A white cup adorned with gold around the rim and a sprig of white flowers inside. A black cup with ornate silver filigree.

The box was full, and I was tired. I taped it shut and stacked it on top of the others waiting to go to the townhome. I'd drive them over tomorrow evening and unpack some of them so I could reuse them.

For now, a shower and bed. Minuit curled up against the back of my knees as I lay listening to Santa Fe falling asleep. Mostly quiet, with the occasional car driving by, distant music, laughter from somewhere, a breath of wind. It would be quieter at the townhome, I thought, and wondered if I would like that.

At 9:15 Saturday morning, a gigantic black Range Rover pulled up behind the tearoom. I was in the kitchen, considering snitching a scone, but they were still in the oven and the person getting out of the Range Rover was Owen. With a hasty farewell to Ramon, I hurried to meet him at the back door.

"Good morning," Owen said, smiling. "Your chariot awaits!"

"That is enormous," I said as he opened the passenger door for me.

"That's what all the girls say."

I gave him a Look. "Boys too, no doubt."

He gave a delighted laugh as I got in, then closed the door and went to the driver's side. "I left the mattress in back, since you said you were picking up antiques," he said as he started the engine.

"Thanks," I said. "The table is sturdy but the chair is less so. And I might need to get a second coffee table, if you have room."

"I bet we do."

Looking over my shoulder, I saw that there were no seats behind me, only a level space all the way to the back, big enough to hold what appeared to be a full-sized mattress. Holy moly, this was a big car!

I directed Owen to the second-hand store. Rick was not there, but a nice older woman who reminded me of a sturdier Claudia Pearson said she'd find my table in the back and bring it out.

"I'm going to look for another one while you do that," I told her.

Owen followed me through the large room full of sofas and (not suitable) arm chairs, to the back where dining tables and other miscellaneous pieces, including coffee tables, were on display. There were two that might do: one a very plain, very rectangular table of oak; the other an oval-shaped table with a rather dark walnut stain that was not quite as large as I'd like.

"Get the round one," Owen suggested. "Look at the legs."

I hadn't noticed them, but now I saw that they were claw legs, ending in lion's paws. "Oh, my!"

"You must have that in Marigold, mustn't you?"

"I think you're right. It's a bit small—"

"Then add an end table. This one might go." Owen picked up a small, round table that was slightly lighter in color and set it next to the coffee table. "Put a bit of lace on it, no one will know they don't match."

The small one could go between two chairs, and was just big enough to hold a couple of place settings. "Yes," I said. "Thank you. Let's find someone—"

"I can carry this one," Owen said, and picked up the oval table, turning it on its side. I lifted the little one and followed him as he edged his way through the aisle. We were nearing the capstan table.

"Owen, stop a minute. You've got to see this!"

Owen set the coffee table down and gave me a curious look. I put the round table beside it, then went to the capstan.

"Very pretty," he said, "but aren't you bringing the dining table from the tearoom?"

"Yes. I'm not getting this one, I just wanted to show it to you."

Wishing Rick was here, I looked around for another employee but there were none nearby. I bent down to look underneath the table, found the locking mechanism, and figured out how it worked.

"Watch this," I said, and gently pulled on the edge of the table. It turned easily, the leaves rising up and unfolding themselves, then slipping into place.

"That. Is. *Fabulous!*" Owen crowed. "I want it!"

"Where would you put it, though?"

"I have no idea," Owen said, looking at the price tag. "Oh, yes. I'm sure it's worth more than this. I must have it!"

"I thought about getting it for a conference table," I said, "but I don't think we could get it upstairs."

"Nonsense! Anything is possible."

Owen knelt to peer at the underside of the table, touching the locking mechanism, then looking at the pedestal. "I believe the top and base can be moved separately."

"May I help you?" said the Claudia-like woman from behind me, making me jump.

Owen stood and gave me a querying look. With a small shake of my head, I turned to the employee, taking note of her name tag, which read "Maureen."

"I'd like these two tables as well," I said, gesturing to the ones I had chosen.

"And I will purchase this set," Owen said, laying a hand on the capstan table.

4

I STIFLED A GASP. *"Owen!"* I hissed.

He glanced at me, grinning. The Claudia clone—Maureen—looked from him to me and back.

"The set includes the chairs," she said, "and the table requires a large truck to move."

"I'm sure it does," Owen said. "I'll arrange for it to be picked up as soon as possible."

"All right." She removed the price tag from the capstan table and started toward the register.

Owen lifted the coffee table and I grabbed the end table, following them to the front, where Owen whipped out a credit card. While Maureen rang up the capstan set, I sorted through a welter of mixed feelings.

I shouldn't be jealous of Owen, but I was. How nice to be able to indulge in expensive and impractical furniture on a whim! I was glad for him, and a little wistful that I hadn't been able to splurge on the thing myself, but really. Even if it *could* be taken up my stairs, I didn't *need* a fancy spinning conference table.

Maureen peered at the tag on the coffee table, about to add it to Owen's bill.

"No, no," I said, indicating my tables. "These two are separate."

She looked at me, then at Owen, then printed out a ticket for him to sign. I dug in my purse for the tearoom's credit card.

"If you don't mind we'll just mark your set 'sold' and leave it on the floor," she said to Owen. "That table is hard to move."

"That's fine," he said. "I'll be in touch about picking it up. Are you open tomorrow?"

"Yes, from noon to six."

"Excellent."

I paid my much less exciting bill for the two smaller tables, then looked around for the cherry coffee table. It was sitting near the front door. Owen picked up the oval table and I the smaller one, and Maureen followed us, collecting the cherry table as we went out.

All three pieces fit easily into the Range Rover. We thanked Maureen and got in.

"Will your chair still fit?" Owen asked. "How big is it?"

I peered over my shoulder into the back. There seemed to be plenty of room. "Not very," I said. "A little bigger than the dining chairs you just bought."

"Oh, it should go, then. Where to?"

I directed him to the antique store, where we retrieved the floral chair without any additional purchases, much to my relief. From a compartment somewhere at the back of the Range Rover, Owen produced a padded quilt to wrap around the chair before tenderly placing it in the back. As he drove toward the tearoom, I glanced at the digital clock on his fancy dashboard for the time: 10:17.

"You're moving the dining table and your bed at what time tomorrow?" Owen asked.

"Around midday," I said.

"Would you be willing to do me an enormous favor?"

"Maybe," I said warily.

"I don't, at the moment, have a place for that capstan set. Would you be willing to store it for me at the tearoom? You're welcome to use it in the meantime."

"Oh, Owen, no!"

"I have friends who can move it. They can get it up the stairs. You don't have to worry about that at all."

"But—"

"Please?"

I gazed at him in dismay. "Tell me that's not why you bought it," I said in a small voice.

Coming to a stop at a red light, he turned his head to look at me. "I bought it because I adore it. It's simply too wonderful to pass up. And since you like it too, I would love to give you the use of it for now."

Feeling guilty, I sighed. It would be churlish of me to refuse, and I didn't want to. Perhaps it would have been better if I hadn't showed Owen the table. I'd merely wanted to share a fun thing with him; I hadn't dreamed he would buy it on the spot. Henceforward, I'd know better.

I swallowed. "I'd be delighted," I said.

"Good!" The light changed, and Owen drove forward. "If I can arrange it, may I have it brought to the tearoom tomorrow afternoon? The friends I mentioned are professional movers; they know how to deal with large furniture. They moved my Steinway for me. They'll take care of everything."

You have a Steinway?

"Um, all right," I said meekly.

"Thanks, Ellen!" He shot a grin at me. "What a great find!"

At the tearoom, Owen helped me bring my purchases upstairs, where I put them with the furniture from Hyacinth. All of it would go downstairs after the dining table had been moved to the townhome.

He then took himself off to round up his moving friends, promising to let me know when the capstan set would be arriving. I saw him out, and stood on the back *portal* watching the Range Rover drive away, trying to collect myself.

What was it I was doing today? Oh, yes. Managing a tearoom.

I went in and made the rounds of the parlors. The servers—Rosa and Iz, this morning, to be joined later by Dale—were putting the finishing touches on the place settings in the alcoves. It was a lovely day, and I'd decided against light-ing fires in the fireplaces. Spring was on its way in.

The gift shop was stocked up and ready. In the kitchen, Ramon had been joined by Hanh, who glanced up from assembling sandwiches as I peeked in. I smiled, then left and went up to my office.

Oh, god, I needed tea. Ai.

The samovar pot was full, I noted, and I thought I detected the smoky aroma of Lapsang Souchong. Lifting the lid, I confirmed this, and added sugar and milk to my cup after I poured.

"I made a fresh pot," Kris said, joining me. "I drank up the first one. Did you look at the ad copy?"

"Not yet. Give me a few minutes."

She went back to her desk, and I went to mine. Resolutely avoiding looking at anything on it, I watched Minuit play with her ring toy as I drank my tea. The Lapsang Souchong was powerful. After one sip I went back and added more milk and sugar. I needed to get some more sour cherries. I'd make a note ... somewhere.

The morning had left me feeling a bit like a refugee adrift on a lifeboat. Owen's generosity was unsettling.

Surely he only meant to be kind. He was indulging himself, not me. Well, also me, but the capstan set was *his*. I'd have to keep reminding myself of that.

My teacup was empty. I refilled it, with extra sugar, and returned to my desk. Kris's ad copy lay in my in-box, and now I perused it. She'd done an excellent job of describing the positions without giving away the tearoom's identity, but I found myself wishing the ads were more interesting. "Part-time to full-time server at elegant local restaurant. Flexible hours, benefits." And, "Gift shop manager, full-time, benefits." And our phone number.

The paper charged by the word, it was true,

but these seemed rather stark.

A knock made me look up. Kris stood in the doorway. "What do you think?"

"They're pretty good," I said, putting the page down, "but let's hold off until after the staff meeting on Tuesday. I want to let them offer ideas."

"Deadline for the Friday paper is Wednesday."

"All right. I'll decide Tuesday."

"Okay." Her hand went to the long necklace of jet beads she always wore. "I'm caught up, mind if I leave?"

"Not at all."

"Thanks. See you Monday."

Minuit had curled up on her little makeshift bed, the towel she had slept on since the night I'd found her shivering outside the back door. I watched her snoozing, tempted to follow suit. Instead I took out a sheet of paper and started making a list of duties for the gift shop manager. Kris was handling most of these tasks, but I didn't want her to have to spend a lot of time bringing the new person up to speed. She was plenty busy without that.

Apart from a couple of visits downstairs to check on things, I stayed at my desk until five. I'd sent one text to Tony, informing him of my plan to unpack some boxes that evening. No response so far.

There was leftover pizza.

Sighing, I got up to make one more round down in the tearoom. Minuit gave a hopeful chirp, but it was too early to feed her. I scritched her instead, then went downstairs.

Some of the guests had left already. Iz and Dale came and went along the hallway, and Rosa was in the shop, ringing up purchases for departing customers. All but two of the heart-shaped boxes had sold, I saw.

Good. One more week, plus a couple of days, until March. If we wanted more "Irish stuff," it was time to order it.

On the back of a lavender message slip, I made a to-do list for Monday.

Irish stuff

sour cherries

more chairs for new alcoves

bring in screens

bit of lace for small table

ornaments, rugs, lamps

Dahlia

And maybe a table and chairs for the staff meeting, if the capstan set didn't arrive by tomorrow. Sunday would be hectic, moving furniture out and then in, or down. Plus Phillips was coming late in the afternoon to extract the pistol ball from the wall. I should wait on moving the alcove furniture into the dining parlor—might not happen until Monday.

Checking my list from Saturday, I added *look at museum courtyard* to the bottom. If I did that, I could honestly tell Gina I'd been looking for a wedding venue.

The tearoom was momentarily silent, enough for me to hear the distant chime of the mantel clock downstairs. Was the sound coming up the chimney? Or just the stairwell? Oddly, I'd never thought about it.

Enough for today. Standing up from my desk, I took Minuit out of her playpen and carried her to my suite. Fed her, changed clothes, grabbed the pizza and stuffed some salad makings into a bag.

Tonight, I'd dine at the new place.

At precisely 10:00 a.m. Sunday morning I heard the rumble of a large vehicle in the driveway below. Minuit stopped rattling her ring toy and froze, listening. I was at my desk, still looking for something wonderful for Dahlia, having already stripped my bed and packed my toiletry bag. Jumping up, I hurried downstairs.

Manny had backed the truck in and opened the doors, and was deploying a ramp to the back *portal* of the tearoom. With him were Nat and his friend Louie Cordova, who was on my "to call" list.

"Mr. Cordova! I didn't know you were coming," I said as I came out of the door.

He nodded, smiling. Wearing a denim jacket over jeans and a flannel shirt, he was short, stocky, and a bit grizzled. He was also, I knew, a master adobe mason.

Manny dropped the end of the ramp on the *portal*. "Got a bed to move, don't you?" he said, dusting his hands. "Gonna need help with the mattress and box springs."

"Yes. You're brilliant, *Tio*."

"Table first," he said.

The table was already collapsed to its smallest, the leaves stacked against the wall of the dining parlor. The chairs were in the hall, out of the way. Captain Dusenberry had not reacted to all this activity, as far as I could tell. No flickering lights, no stereo coming on.

I'd done all that the previous night. Having unpacked some boxes at the townhome and loaded them back in my car; made salad and reheated the pizza in the nifty, slender oven that was tucked in above the regular oven; consumed them at Tony's small, round dinette table in a bow window off the kitchen; and wandered around the mostly-empty house for a while, I had given up on seeing Tony. There was evidence of his presence in the form of dirty dishes in the dishwasher and laundry strewn around the den, where he was sleeping on my father's sofa bed, but he still hadn't answered my text.

Manny and Louie moved the dining table into the truck. Nat and I followed with the leaves, and there was much deployment of padded coverings and strategic tiedowns. We then all trooped upstairs to disassemble the canopy frame from the bed. Manny and Louie did the heavy furniture lifting, carrying the mattress and box spring down the stairs (which were blessedly wide in this old house) while Nat and I hovered, watching to make sure nothing hit the wall or the banister. Then the dresser, bed frame, canopy frame, and finally all the dining chairs were packed into Manny's truck. I packed the freshly-laundered canopy hangings into a box and put it in my trunk.

Toward the end of all this, I turned on an oven in the downstairs kitchen and baked up some scones, and made some of Julio's coffee to go with. I served them at the kitchen break table.

"Made good time," Manny remarked, stirring sugar into his coffee.

"I can't thank you all enough," I said.

Nat smiled. "We're only halfway done. Wait until we're finished."

Louie lifted the spoon from the lemon curd and peered at it.

"It's lemon curd," I told him. "It's sort of a spread."

He nodded and put the spoon back. I demonstrated, adding curd and a dollop of cream to one half of my scone. He smiled, and bit into his without amendments.

"Mr. Cordova, I'd like to hire you to do some repairs on the wall in the dining parlor," I said.

His grizzled eyebrows rose. "Looks okay to me."

"Well, I'm having—uh, an artifact—removed from it later today, and it will need repair."

"It's adobe, no?"

"Yes."

"I can look at it, but not today."

"At your convenience. Tomorrow would be good, or any morning before ten."

He agreed to come by in the morning and give me an estimate. I poured the last of the coffee into their cups, hastily tidied the kitchen, and fetched my purse and keys. I'd be leading Manny to the townhome, with Nat accompanying me in my car.

"I see you got another low table," Nat commented.

"Yes, I realized we needed one for Marigold."

"It's lovely. The new alcoves are going to be splendid!"

I smiled, but my thoughts were not on the new alcoves. They were sneaking ahead to the afternoon, because Owen had texted me that the capstan set would be coming at two o'clock.

Unloading the furniture at the townhome went faster, though Manny and Louie had to edge the dining table through the front door carefully. I put the leaves on some storage shelves in the garage, and the extra chairs against the dining room wall, where they looked like soldiers awaiting a call to duty. The bed was reassembled without incident and looked great in the master bedroom, although a bit barren without the canopy hangings. I had only one nightstand, unfortunately. Maybe I'd find another when I went hunting for more tearoom furniture.

"Gonna take off," Manny said, folding up a padded blanket. "Got a game this afternoon."

I thanked them all, gave them tearoom gift cards, and told Mr. Cordova I looked forward to seeing him on Monday. When the truck had disappeared down the street, I went back into the townhome.

The dining room seemed a little crowded with all ten chairs. Maybe I'd put some in the garage. I should ask Tony.

When I saw him again. Hopefully in this lifetime.

Sighing, I found my purse and checked my phone. Lo and behold, a text!

> Sorry, babe. We're on a roll, couldn't stop. See you tonight.

Well, yes—sooner or later he had to sleep, and I'd see him then. In a fit of optimism, I texted back:

> Should I make dinner?

Out of what? If he said yes, I'd have to hit the grocery store. Not much was left in my mini-fridge at the tearoom. I checked my watch.

After one-forty. Time to head back.

I arrived at the tearoom to find another large truck—this one painted black with "Manifesto" on the side in elaborate silver script—parked in my space. Owen's Mercedes was behind the kitchen; I parked beside it and hurried to open the back door. Owen himself was lounging on the bench near the lilacs, while two very large men in black jeans and black leather jackets stood at the back of the truck, which was open. Owen got up and joined them as I unlocked the door.

"Sorry," I said. "I was at the townhome."

"No problem," Owen said. "We just got here a few minutes ago. Ellen, this is Jerry and Don. You might have seen them at the Masquerade."

I nodded and smiled. "Hello."

I did not recall them from the masquerade, but there had been fifty-odd people in attendance, and they would have been in costume. They looked very professional today, though not what I would have expected from movers. More like—I don't know, hit men, maybe.

They also looked interchangeable. Both had pierced ears with silver studs. Both wore black sunglasses. Both had short, black hair. Jerry's looked like it might want to curl if it was longer.

I found the doorstop and propped the back door open for the second time that day. "Come on in."

"Where does it go?" Jerry said, walking through the door and looking around the hall.

"Upstairs. I'll show you."

I led the way upstairs, where I had moved the new tea tables and all the Hyacinth furnishings out of the way, leaving a space to the west of the door to my suite that ought to be big enough for the capstan set. Jerry stood in the middle of it, looking around at the upper hall.

"Uh-huh," he said, nodding. "Okay, let's do it."

He and Don went down the stairs, followed

by Owen. I was about to bring up the rear when a plaintive "mew" stopped me.

"Minuit! Don't worry, honey, it's all right."

I went into my office and gave the kitten a quick cuddle and a couple of treats, then went back downstairs. Owen was back on the *portal,* watching the movers slowly roll a large lump swathed in padding blankets—which must be the table's massive pedestal—down the ramp on a dolly.

Impulse prompted me to make another pot of coffee. I went into the kitchen and did so, then set out mugs, spoons, cream and sugar. Returning to the hall, I saw Jerry and Don taking the pedestal up the lower flight of the stairs. On the landing they conferred briefly, moved the dolly to the foot of the upper flight, and started up again.

"Do I smell coffee?" Owen asked. He was standing in the doorway to the main parlor, also watching.

"Yes. Would you like some?"

"Please."

We went into the kitchen and I poured mugs for both of us, adding sugar and cream to mine. I was hungry—I hadn't had lunch. Muffled thumps and muffled voices could be heard overhead.

"They must be very strong," I commented,

glancing toward the ceiling. "I don't think I could lift that with one other person."

"Oh, yeah," Owen said, both hands wrapped around his mug. "They're bodybuilders. They're also meticulous."

"Hello?" called a voice from out in the hall.

We went out and found Jerry at the foot of the stairs. Don was headed out the back door with a stack of folded padded blankets.

"Can you come look at where we've put the foot?" Jerry asked. "If you want it in a different place, now's the time."

"Okay."

Owen and I followed him upstairs. The pedestal stood gleaming in the middle of the upper hall. Now that it wasn't hidden by the top, I saw that it, too, was made of absolutely beautiful wood. Apart from a few bits of metal, including four stout pins rising from the center, it was all polished wood. The turning mechanism must all be in the table top.

I stood by the door to my suite, visualizing how the table would look when expanded and surrounded by the chairs. "A couple more feet toward the window would be good," I said. That would ensure that the chairs weren't in front of the suite door.

Jerry nodded as Don came back up the stairs. Together they shifted the table pedestal, then

Jerry looked at me for approval.

"Yes," I said. "That looks good."

They headed down again, with Owen and me close behind. As we all rounded the stairs and headed for the back door, Don paused.

"Smells like coffee," he remarked, head tilted upward like a hound scenting its quarry.

"Yes," I said. "Would you like some?"

"Maybe later," Jerry said, and they both went out again.

Owen and I watched while they brought the table top—also swathed in padding—out of the truck. This time they were using a kind of sling that went around their shoulders and cradled the round top on its side. Fascinated, I watched them carry it up the stairs. With their hands free to steady the table top, one going backward, they traded places on the landing. They went much more quickly than Manny and Louie had done. That table top had to be heavy, with all the leaves and the turning mechanism. They made moving it look easy.

Upstairs they unwrapped the top and carefully positioned it on the pedestal. Jerry set a bubble level on it and peered closely at it while Don went back downstairs. He returned in a minute with a small tool kit, and secured the table top to the pedestal. When he was finished, Jerry crouched down and peered at his work, then unlatched the lock and stood. With a gentle pull, he set the table in motion. It unfolded and settled into its larger shape without a hitch.

I let out my breath in a sigh. I hadn't realized I was holding it.

The table was magnificent.

Don began folding up the padding materials while Jerry took the toolkit downstairs. I stepped toward the table, touching its beautiful surface, hardly believing it was here.

"Looks great up here," Owen said, joining me.

"Yes."

"Thanks for giving me a place to stash it."

"You'll let me know when you have a place to *use* it," I reminded him.

He nodded. "That's the plan."

Jerry came back up carrying a swaddled chair. In a short while, all ten chairs were upstairs, unwrapped, and standing around the table. There was just enough room to walk past it on all sides, and the suite's door was not blocked.

Jerry came over to where Owen and I stood. "All good?"

"Yes." I nodded. "Thank you."

"Send me your bill," Owen said.

"Right. Later, man," Jerry said, giving Owen a fist bump. "Ma'am," he added, with a glance at me.

He and Don went downstairs, and Owen and I followed. They were already in the truck when I realized I'd forgotten to offer them coffee. I refilled Owen's and my mugs as they rumbled away down the driveway.

"How'd the moving go this morning?" Owen asked.

"Fine. I still need to put the hangings back on the bed."

And empty my desk—*that* still had to be moved. Having failed my ambition to get the office packed up as well as my bedroom, I'd decided it would get moved later. Kris and I could probably manage the chaise longue. I might ask Tony for help with the desk and the credenza.

"Big changes," Owen remarked.

"Yes."

Leaning against the kitchen counter, I peered into my coffee and thought about all the changes that had happened in the last few days. Physical changes, mostly, but they were inextricably tied to my emotions, because they impacted my both my business and my personal life so strongly.

Tonight, I'd begin living with Tony. One step —a big one—closer to marriage.

The sound of a vehicle on the driveway made me turn to look out the window. An SUV pulled up and parked at the back door. My parking space was busy today.

"Ah, already?" I said, glancing at the clock.

"Problem?" Owen asked.

"No, no. I just—I need to grab some groceries for dinner. I'll do it after Phillips is done."

Owen finished his coffee and set his mug near the coffee pot. "Done with what? If it's none of my business, just say so."

"He's going to take a pistol ball out of the wall, I hope. I might have mentioned it."

Owen faced me, leaning a hip against the counter. "No, I don't think you did. How did the pistol ball get there?"

"We *think* it may be the ball that killed Captain Dusenberry."

"Oh, wow!" He grinned. "How cool is that! Can I watch?"

"If Phillips doesn't mind." The sound of a car door being closed reached us. I finished my coffee and put down the mug. "I'd better go let him in."

Owen tagged along as I opened the kitchen's back door and stepped out. Phillips was getting a couple of large cases out of the back of the SUV. Dee, standing by the passenger door in jeans and a cream-colored sweater, waved and started toward us.

"Hi, Ellen! Hi, Owen. Taking pictures?"

Owen smiled. "Not today."

"Just observing? Me too."

Phillips came up, carrying his gear. "Afternoon," he said cheerfully.

"Hi," I said, opening the door to the hall for him. "Thanks for coming."

"My pleasure." He paused, tilting his head and looking at Owen. "We've met."

Owen gave a nod. "Last October."

"Oh, right. The photographer."

"Yes. Mind if I observe?"

Phillips shrugged. "Fine with me." He went in and through the door to the dining parlor, stopping in the middle. "Table's gone."

"Yes," I said. "Oh, sorry—I have a folding table if you need a work space."

"Nah, that's okay." He put the cases on the floor near the fireplace, knelt, and opened one.

Dee, Owen, and I watched while Phillips got out his smaller metal detection tool and verified the spot on the wall where he wanted to work, then used an electric drill to attach a large, black ring to the wall over the spot with long screws. I winced at the sound of them going into the wall, knowing there'd be worse to come.

Phillips opened the other case and removed what looked sort of like a bigger electric drill, with a long, tube-like attachment. He put them together, creating a tool that reminded me of a science-fiction ray gun. Dee plugged it in for him.

"This is the core drill," he told me, showing me the tube, which was about four inches in diameter. "It's going to make a pretty big hole. That's so I can remove the ball without damaging it."

I nodded. "I've got repairs lined up."

"Great."

Phillips put on work gloves and ear protectors, then took two pairs of safety goggles out of one of the cases, put one on over his glasses, and handed the other to Dee. "You might want to stand back," he told me and Owen. "Sorry, I don't have more goggles."

"It's okay," I said, moving across the room to the French doors. Owen joined me, taking out his phone and composing a text.

Phillips lined up the end of the tube against the wall through the ring, then started it. The core drill was loud and moved very slowly. I began to wish for a chair. I'd been on my feet a *lot* today.

And I still hadn't had lunch. Argh.

My stomach grumbled at the reminder. I ignored it and watched Phillips work, wondering if his arms were getting tired. Finally he turned the drill off and slowly pulled it back, then set it on the floor and took off his ear protectors.

"Unplug it, Dee."

She did so, and Phillips extracted the core from the tube. It was a cylindrical chunk of adobe about eight inches long. Laying it on the floor, he aimed the metal-detecting pen-thing at it, sweeping it slowly along the length. The pen-thing gave a chirp.

"Got it. Right there." He pointed at a spot about two thirds of the way along the core, then got out a pen and marked it.

"Oh!" I said, stepping forward for a closer look. There was nothing to see, but I couldn't help myself.

Phillips picked up the core, looked closely at its surface, and rubbed at one end with his gloved fingers. A little dust came off, but not much.

"Safest thing for the artifact is to dissolve the adobe. I'll take it to the lab and do that. Sorry I can't just break it open and show you."

"No, no," I said. "That's fine. Do what's best for the ball."

"It'll take a while to dissolve. I might have something for you tomorrow evening."

"That would be great. Thank you so much!"

He smiled and picked up the electric drill, with which he removed the black ring from the wall. One large hole and four smaller ones remained. Phillips began packing up his gear.

Remembering the coffee, I offered him some,

and he accepted. Dee came to the kitchen, poured two mugs and added sugar to one and cream to the other, and carried them back out. I glanced at Owen, who had followed along. He was looking at his phone, then looked up at me.

"I'll get out of your way," he said, putting the phone in his pocket. "Thanks for letting me stay. It was fascinating."

I nodded and poured the last of the coffee into my mug.

"By the way, Julio and I would like you and Tony to join us for dinner tonight. Nothing fancy."

"Oh—thank you!"

He smiled. "You've had a long day. Figured you might not want to cook."

I nodded. "I'm pretty tired. Yes, I'll come. I don't know whether Tony will. I'll text him."

"Six o'clock okay?"

"Fine," I said, taking out my phone. "Thank you, Owen. And tell Julio thanks, too."

"See you soon. Thanks for the coffee."

He left. I sent Tony a text about dinner, then remained in the kitchen, washing the coffee things and thinking about the day. Dee came in with two empty mugs and washed them herself, then got out the vacuum we used to tidy the tearoom and carried it to the dining parlor to clean up the small amount of debris made by the core drill. Phillips had packed up his gear and was loading it into the SUV.

"I'll text you some photos as soon as I have something," he said, coming back in while Dee was putting away the vacuum.

"Thanks. Will you send me a bill for your time?"

He smiled, sliding an arm around Dee's waist as she returned. "Nah, this is fun. Good experience, too—I've never drilled an adobe core before."

We all said goodbye and I saw them out, locking the back door behind them, then went back into the dining parlor. How strange to see it empty again, except for a couple of sideboards against the walls and some ornaments on the mantel. The gaping hole near the fireplace was distressing; I'd bring in a screen to hide it. To-morrow.

With the dining table gone, I could more easily picture this room as Captain Dusenberry's study. Desk by the north windows, facing south, according to our theory about the pistol ball. I looked forward to seeing if that was indeed what Phillips had just removed from the wall.

Into the silence fell a familiar half dozen notes from the piano in the main parlor: the opening phrase of "Contessa Perdono." I closed my eyes and exhaled, then looked up at the chandelier.

One crystal drop moving slightly.

The next six notes played. *Perdono, perdono.* Forgive me, forgive me.

Could he be asking my forgiveness, concerned by the removal of the furniture?

Or could he be asking Maria's forgiveness, for being unable to see their elopement through? Was he caught here in the memories, the hopes they had shared of a lifetime together? How very sad, if that was so.

With a deep sigh, I said, "If you want my forgiveness, you have it."

Silence. The crystal had fallen still.

5

I WAITED FOR SEVERAL MINUTES, but the Captain played no more on the piano, and the chandelier remained motionless. Outside the French doors, the evening light was slanting, casting long shadows of the bare-branched trees along the driveway. Finally I went upstairs to collect Minuit and my toiletries.

She started calling as soon as she heard me on the stairs. Poor little kitty—so much noise and chaos! If I'd planned it better I would have moved her over to the new place in the morning. I took her out of the playpen and cuddled her as I turned to look at the upper hall.

The capstan table stood proudly encircled by all its chairs, fitting the space as if made for it. As it happened, the upstairs chandelier lined up perfectly with its center. Boy, would our staff meetings be elegant!

Of course, there was a clutter of furniture for the new alcoves shoved up against the wall. I'd deal with that tomorrow. Fishing my keys out of my pocket, I unlocked my suite—no longer my suite. The bedroom looked strange, empty as it was. Oddly, it looked smaller, perhaps because the sloping ceiling was now more visible.

"Mew," Minuit said.

"Yeah. Let's get you moved, sweetie."

This involved a fair amount of work, including emptying the litter boxes and packing up her playpen, toys, and food. I gave her supper to keep her busy while I did all that and carried things down to my car. When I returned from the final trip, I found her standing in the middle of the empty bedroom. She looked up at me with a small, forlorn mew.

"You're going to like the new place better, promise," I told her.

I washed her bowl and put her in her carrier, then locked the suite (Why? Habit.) and carried her downstairs. She cried all through the short drive; she didn't like riding in the car, even in her comfy carrier.

I took her into the townhome and set up her litter box in the laundry room and her playpen in the master bedroom, then put her in the playpen. I didn't want her exploring unsupervised while I was at dinner, and it was almost six.

Taking out my phone, I walked over to the French doors in the bedroom. The sun was approaching the western horizon, and Santa Fe was already beginning to light up. Tony hadn't responded to my text. With a sigh, I put away my phone and went to find the box with the canopy hangings for the bed. I'd have to make the bed, too, but that could wait until after dinner.

Monday morning, I woke up alone in my bed. The room was abnormally bright, and it took me a minute to realize why. Turning over on my back, I saw a glow of morning light from the French doors filling the room. I'd have to mount some drapes over them. In winter, the sun might get far enough south to shine directly in.

Tony hadn't joined us for dinner. Nor had he joined me in the hot tub, where I had drunk the last bit of whiskey as I soaked my tired body in solitude. It felt blissfully good, and made me sleepy. I put on pajamas and made the bed, then fell into it.

Had to get up again at once, to release Minuit from her playpen in response to her strong complaints. Fell back into bed, and knew no more until morning. There had been a couple of thumps during the night, so Tony must have come home, but I hadn't fully awakened.

Was this how it was going to be? Not all the time, surely. Or even most of the time, I hoped. Because otherwise, I wasn't sure it would work.

With a frustrated sigh, I turned my head to look at what I already thought of as Tony's pillow. There was a Minuit-shaped impression in it, but she was gone. I glanced at the clock: 8:16. Ai! I was late! Good thing it was Monday.

Feeling disinclined to dress up, especially since I would be moving furniture, I skipped the dresses I had carefully hung in my closet and dug in the boxes I had not yet unpacked until I found slacks and a pretty sweater. Walking down the hall to the kitchen I encountered Minuit sniffing at the crack under the closed door to Tony's room. She looked up at me with a hopeful mew.

"Sorry. I don't think he wants you in there."

I fed her, then put some water in my electric kettle and turned it on. I'd have just one cup of tea here before going over to the tearoom.

After a cursory look in the fridge and the cupboards, I poured myself a bowl of Tony's cereal for breakfast, put it on the table, then hunted for a notepad and pen to make a grocery list. I found them in the little mini-desk cubby near the door into the garage, and there was a note from Tony scrawled on the pad:

*Didn't want to wake you. See you
tonight.*

Promising, but I wasn't going to hold my breath. At times, Tony's job ate his life.

I made my cup of tea and drank it while I made a list—mostly staples: flour, sugar, more cereal, more milk, cream, butter, bread, eggs, some cheese and deli turkey, stuff for salad. Enough for me, and presumably Tony, to survive on without eating out all the time. If I was going to be cooking dinner on a regular basis I'd need to start making meal plans, but it looked like that wasn't going to be an issue this week.

I ate the cereal (uninteresting), tidied up, and found my coat. The list went into my purse; I'd pick all that up on the way home from the tearoom. With a farewell scritch for Minuit, who had shadowed me from room to room, I headed off to work.

The tearoom stood bathed in morning light, a sight I hadn't seen often. Even the back of the house was pretty, the gentle blue of the pitched roof contrasting with warm beige adobe walls and the white frames of the windows and doors. Smiling, I went in through the kitchen door so I could say good morning to Julio and Hanh.

Hanh was putting flour into the big mixer.

Julio was at the stove, creating something. Interesting savory aromas filled the room: onion, sage, some kind of cheese toasting.

"Ten o'clock?" I asked him, peeking over his shoulder into a pan of simmering onions.

He nodded, and I got out of the way. Upstairs I found that Kris had turned on the samovar and made a pot of Keemun, for which I was grateful, though I was a little embarrassed that she'd arrived before me. Resolving to do better from now on, poked my head into her office to say hello.

"Morning," Kris replied, and nodded toward the hall. "Where'd you get the table?"

"Ah—well, it's not mine. It's Owen's."

She gave me a quizzical look. "Oh?"

I poured myself a cup of tea, sat in her guest chair, and gave her the whole story. By the end of it she was looking amused.

"Yeah, that's Owen's M.O. If you're not careful, he'll give it to you permanently."

"I know. I won't let him. But come see how it works."

We went out to the hall and I demonstrated collapsing the table. "That *is* pretty awesome," she said. "Can I try?"

I nodded. She opened it easily.

"We'll keep it closed most of the time, I think," I said. "You and I can use it for lunch if we're eating in. I thought I'd leave it open for now, since we have a staff meeting tomorrow."

The phone rang, and Kris went back to her desk. I refilled my teacup and settled at my own desk to check my messages. After dealing with the ones requiring immediate attention, I went down to pull screens out of the shed.

The first one went in front of the hole that Phillips had made. Four others I stacked against the wall, to be set up after the furniture was in. While I was bringing them in, Louie Cordova arrived to look at the hole in the wall. I moved the screen aside.

"Uh-huh," he said, peering at the hole and touching the wall. "Should be easy to fix. When do you want me to come?"

"Maybe next Monday?"

He agreed, quoted me a price that sounded fair, and we shook hands. I saw him out, then checked my phone.

Almost ten. The rest could wait until after my meeting with Julio.

I nipped upstairs and fetched my travel mug from my suite, emptied the samovar teapot into it, started a fresh pot and dropped the timer on Kris's desk, then grabbed a notebook and pen and went down to the kitchen.

Hanh glanced up from the work table where she was cutting scones as I came in. I smiled, then went to the break table. Julio was waiting for me there, with several small plates holding things for me to taste. Usually there were only a couple, but I had asked him for special items to add on St. Patrick's Day. My mouth started watering at the sight of them.

He gave me a printed copy of his draft menu for March, and we went over it together. The savories all sounded good—watercress and cucumber sandwiches, shepherd's pie, mushroom and onion pasties—none so exotic that I felt I should try them before approving them. For the special bread, Julio offered me an orangeish scone. On the plate beside it was a small shamrock piped out of butter.

"Cheddar scone," he said. "The butter is optional, but we usually offer condiments with the breads."

"Well, it looks adorable." I tried a bite of the scone without butter. "Oh, Julio—that's *fabulous!*"

He smiled as I put a dab of the butter on my second bite. "It's pretty easy," he said. "I had to tweak the recipe. The cheese pretty much takes the place of the butter."

"Mmm."

He offered me a taste of an Irish Butter Tea Cake, simple and delicious. The other sweets would be apple pie and a ginger snap. It was a lovely, hearty menu and a nice contrast from the more delicate February menu.

"Now, these are the ideas for additions for St. Patrick's Day." He set a plate before me with a miniature sandwich on it: two, maybe three bites. Looked like rye bread.

"Corned beef?" I said, picking it up and trying a small bite. An unexpected medley of flavors filled my mouth: sauerkraut and Swiss cheese and something spicy in addition to the corned beef. "Mm!"

"Yeah, it's a Reuben," Julio said. "I used a remoulade instead of thousand island, but if that's too hot I can go back."

"No, it's wonderful! Oh, man, I want this for lunch."

He smiled, and pushed another plate toward me. "Soda bread."

Resisting the temptation to gobble the rest of the Reuben, I put it down and tried the soda bread. Not usually my favorite bread, but this one was nice and light with a sprinkling of currants. I spread some of the shamrock butter on it.

"If it's too similar to our cream scones, we could leave the currants out," Julio said.

"But I like the currants! It would be pretty plain without them."

"Another option would be to replace the

cream scones with this for the month."

"Good idea! Let's do that. Oh—but for cream tea, as well?"

"I thought we weren't going to be doing cream tea."

"We've got a few reservations that we're going to go ahead and honor, and we're going to offer it for carryout."

"Ah. Well we can make some scones, too. Not difficult."

"Good. People will still want to buy scones from the pastry case. Maybe offer a choice, for the cream tea?"

"Sure."

He picked up the final plate and set it before me. On it was a little round cookie-looking thing with a peak of stiff whipped cream on top.

"Oat cake," he said. "Actually Scottish, but I think we can get away with it."

I picked it up and turned it this way and that. It held together, and the cream didn't slop around. Not messy to eat. When I took a bite it was more delicate than I expected, with a buttery sweetness that was the perfect base for the cream, which had a little whiskey kick.

"Irish whiskey in the cream?" I asked.

"Yes."

"Perfect." I brazenly ate the rest of it. "Yes, that's lovely. Can we do them all?"

"Sure, especially if we sub in the soda bread for the cream scone. The sandwich is the most expensive item. The cream doesn't take a whole lot of whiskey."

"Let's do it. Let Kris know how much to bump the price for St. Patrick's to cover the additions."

"Will do."

We kicked around a few ideas for the April menu, which would be the tearoom's first anniversary. I nibbled the rest of the samples while we talked, starting with the Reuben which I unabashedly devoured. When we had discussed all the ideas we had so far, I thanked Julio and went back upstairs, checked my desk, then turned to the task of setting up the alcoves.

Rugs first: two small ones from the former Poppy and Hyacinth went into Lilac and the new Hyacinth. Then the tables, one of the green wing chairs from my suite for Lilac until I could get something else, the Hyacinth chairs, and finally the Hyacinth screen.

Next: Poppy (mach 2) and Marigold (mach 2). The chairs were in the ground floor hall, so I didn't have to carry them down the stairs, yay! My legs were getting tired already.

When I had the chairs situated, I set up two screens between them to make the corridor to Lilac and Hyacinth. The screens would be replaced by the new drapes, but for now we'd be able to use the alcoves.

I was tired, but I was almost done with this part. I brought down the tables for Poppy and Marigold. The new alcoves looked sparse, especially the larger two, but they were beginning to take shape. Some ornaments would help. I'd go raid my storage unit in the afternoon, but I was ready for a break.

Taking out my phone, I found a text from Gina and oh! It was past noon. No wonder I was hungry.

The thought of food brought my awareness to the mouth-watering smells that pervaded the hall. I followed my nose to the kitchen, where my dreams had come true: a plate holding three full-sized Reubens sat on the break table.

Julio glanced up from washing utensils as I came in. "Ready for lunch?"

"Oh, yeah! *Thank* you, Julio!"

"Hey, we had the ingredients. Might as well use 'em." He moved to the table and invited me to serve myself with a wave of his hand.

"Are you joining us, Hanh?" I called.

"I brought my lunch," she said, putting the lid on a container of scones, then picking it up and taking it to the freezer.

"Well, you're welcome to sit with us if you like."

"The other sandwich is for Kris, if she wants it," Julio said, taking a seat across from me.

I called Kris and informed her that she did indeed want the sandwich awaiting her. Before putting away my phone, I glanced at Gina's text:

> How did you and Tony like
> Hyde Park?

Hyde Park. Oops.

Well, Tony wouldn't have been able to come. I'd answer later. Meanwhile, I helped myself to a Reuben and dug in.

"Mm. Oh." I swallowed a bite. "Julio, you'll want to add this to your menu."

He nodded, mouth full.

Hanh got out her lunch—a bento box of rice and veggies—and joined us at the table, where she demonstrated skillful use of her chopsticks. Evidence was mounting that she was a vegetarian.

Note to self: don't offer Hanh corned beef.

Kris came in, saying, "I looked in the dining parlor. It's looking good. Are you going to get more chairs?"

I nodded. "We'll start with what we have. Two in each alcove is enough for cream tea, probably."

"You could use some of the chairs from the

conference table until you get more comfy chairs," she said, sitting next to Julio and helping herself to a sandwich.

"Good idea," I said.

Hanh looked up. "Conference table?"

Julio shot me a grin. Owen had told him, no doubt.

"Yes," I told Hanh. "We have a new table upstairs. We'll use it for the staff meeting tomorrow."

She gave a nod and continued eating. I'd better post a note by the time clock about the meeting being upstairs, so the staff would see it when they checked in tomorrow morning.

Always something more to do.

After lunch I thanked Julio again with a hug, then got my coat and purse and drove to my storage unit. The sky had clouded over, and a brisk breeze had kicked up. Maybe we'd get some rain. It *smelled* like rain as I got out of my car and dug out the key to the unit. I left the door open for light and went in.

A whiff of dust was swept away by rain-scent from the doorway. I stood in the middle, where Dad's sleeper sofa had been, and looked around. There were a couple of boxes of nick-knacks, I knew. I just needed to find them. Near the back, I spotted the big boxes marked CHINA.

Oh, right. Mom's china. Well, not right now,

but I did want to take it to the townhome. Maybe Owen would help. The boxes looked like they might fit in my Camry...one at a time.

Never mind. I turned slowly, looking at each object until I figured out what it was. A little end table that had been in Dad's study would do for one of the alcoves—probably Poppy, as it was slightly oriental-looking and would go with the cranes screen. I put it in the Camry's back seat, as it was too tall for the trunk.

A four-foot-tall, skinny wooden case that had once held Mom's collection of CDs might make a nice display for some pretty teacups, or some other little gewgaws. Back seat as well.

Still hadn't found the ornaments, but a small rolled rug bundled in plastic caught my eye. I brushed the dust off the top and recognized the rug—a runner that had been in a short hallway in my parents' house. Perfect for the passage back to Lilac and Hyacinth! I put it in the car.

Behind the garden furniture was a stack of smallish boxes, two of which were labeled "ornaments." Bingo! I put them in the trunk and took a last look around for anything that might be useful for the alcoves. There was an arts-and-crafts table lamp that had been Dad's, with a mica lamp shade. Very pretty, but it didn't go with any of the alcoves. Still, it brought back fond memories.

Maybe Tony would like it. I put it in the car.

I had enough of a jumble to deal with for now, and I was starting to get caught up in reminiscing, so I locked the storage unit and returned to the tearoom. The end table went into Poppy, the skinny display case into Marigold, and I unwrapped the runner on the back portal, leaving the dusty bag outside to deal with later.

The rug fit perfectly in the space between Poppy and Marigold. Poppy now had two end tables, so I moved the thrift store one to Marigold.

That left the ornaments. I brought the boxes in and sat in my green chair in Lilac to go through them.

Memories wafted up as I unwrapped tissue paper from the items. The first box contained an iridescent glass globe in shades of purple and blue, a black-on-black pot from San Ildefonso Pueblo (probably valuable—I'd take it to the townhome), an amber-hued stained-glass snail with a light inside, and a ceramic rose blossom, white with yellow edges.

The snail had been Mom's night light. I remembered gazing at it as I fell asleep after seeking refuge from nightmares in her arms.

In the second box were a small bronze stag sitting on the ground with its little forelegs tucked beneath its chest, a round box covered with red and gold beads (Poppy, for sure), a pair of bookends in the form of busts of a Grecian-looking man and woman, a lotus-shaped candle holder, and a white ceramic statuette of an Asian-looking woman.

Ah, yes. Kwan Yin, the Iron Goddess of Mercy. She might go on my desk—I wasn't sure I wanted to share her with the tearoom guests, and risk her possibly being broken.

The rose and the candle holder went into Hyacinth, the globe into lilac, the beaded box and one of the busts into Poppy, the snail and the other bust into Marigold. The little stag fit perfectly on top of the skinny case.

I'd been thinking about putting teacups in that case. We had some chipped ones from the gift shop—unsellable, but perfectly good for decorations—that would do for now. I dug them out from under the displays, unwrapped them, and put one in each little shelf. The result was charming.

The alcoves still looked sparse. They would need more décor and furniture, but there were now a few homey touches in each. Good enough for starters.

Poppy was looking pretty good, with its screen, chairs, and beaded standing lamp. Hadn't there been a teapot we used as a vase?

Yes! There were other ornaments too, from

Poppy and Hyacinth, in boxes somewhere. The storeroom, maybe? I'd find them.

Glancing out the window, I saw that it was now raining—a gentle, soaking rain. Good for the garden.

I checked my phone and was surprised to see that it was after four. I had two more texts from Gina, about our lunch the next day. I texted back:

> Didn't get to Hyde Park.
> See you tomorrow.

I tidied up the boxes and wrappings, fetched the rug bag from the back *portal* and gave it a good hard shake before bringing it in (fortunately the *portal* roof had kept the rain off it), then went upstairs, taking Kwan Yin with me.

I set her on the little café table in my suite, poured myself a cup of tea, and sat there to drink it, watching the rain fall on the garden south of the house. The roses and cottonwoods were still bare-branched, and the lawn had not yet greened up, but in a month I knew it would all be different. Everything would be green and the wisteria would be blooming. I sighed with anticipatory pleasure.

The remainder of the afternoon was spent searching for the ornaments from Hyacinth and Poppy. They were not in the storeroom, nor in my office credenza, nor in the cupboards under the gift shop tables. I finally unearthed them from the bottom storage shelf under the pastry case, where they had been shoved behind a stack of take-out boxes.

The stained-glass table lamp from Hyacinth was there, too, which gave each of the alcoves a pretty light source: table lamps in Hyacinth and Lilac, standing lamp in Poppy, snail in Marigold. Still needed something special for Dahlia, but that was less urgent.

Kris, Julio, and Hanh had all gone home. With a small shock, I realized it was time for *me* to go home, too.

I went upstairs just to make sure there were no emergencies in my in box, though Kris would have told me if there were. I did find a to-do list, mostly about the new alcoves, but at the bottom of it was "Agenda for staff meeting." Gah! Well, I'd do it first thing in the morning. Maybe I'd make some notes tonight. At home.

It felt strange to close my suite after shutting down the samovar. Downstairs I paused for a final peek into the dining parlor: I could see into Marigold and Poppy, and down the passage to Lilac and Hyacinth, from the door. Very similar now to the layout of the main parlor. It would be a good change.

I locked up and drove home. Grateful for the garage, because it was still raining, I parked and carried the mica lamp and the little San Ildefonso pot into the house.

Minuit greeted me at the door, stridently criticizing me for leaving her alone all day. I put the lamp and pot on the kitchen table and picked her up for a cuddle.

Which did I want more? Dinner or a soak in the hot tub? My body was tired, but also hungry. Maybe the rain would stop while I ate.

Setting Minuit down, I dealt with her needs, then put a pot of water on the stove to boil. I got out a second pot and made a simple marinara sauce with a can of tomatoes and some garlic. While it was cooking down, I texted Tony:

> Making dinner.

No response.

Okay. I'd put his share in the fridge, if he didn't show up. I put together a salad while the pasta cooked, then moved the mica lamp into Tony's room; it looked great on his coffee table. I left it on for him, chased out Minuit who had followed me in, and closed the door.

The little black pot went into a *nicho* in the still-empty living room. We needed furniture there, too. I was starting to get burned out on furniture hunting. Maybe Tony would have ideas.

With a bottle of red wine that I'd brought

from my suite, a brocade placemat and even a candle on the table, I was ready for dinner. Minuit wandered through as I dined in elegant solitude.

Afterward I made a few notes for the staff meeting agenda: look at the new alcoves, think about anyone they knew who might like a job as a server or gift shop manager. I'd have to phrase it so they knew that they could apply for the gift shop job if they wanted. I doubted any of them would want it. What else? St. Patrick's. We could use an extra server that day. If we were lucky we'd have a new one on the team by then.

Enough. Time for a soak. I poured myself more wine and took it out to the tub.

The rain had stopped and a chill breeze had come up. The full moon was riding high over the mountains, darting between shreds of cloud. I watched it as I drank my wine, then went inside.

Shower, wash dishes, then bed. I untied the drapes on the side of my bed near the French doors and pulled them together, hoping they'd protect me from the morning sunlight.

Minuit curled up against my calves. I read for a bit, then turned out the light and went to sleep.

I was roused not by daylight, but by the sensation of being watched. Holding my breath, I listened.

It was dark and still. Minuit was a warm spot

against my leg, asleep. I heard a small sound, like a footstep of someone trying to be silent.

"Tony?"

"Sorry," he said. "Didn't mean to wake you."

I turned on my bedside lamp and blinked against the brightness. Tony came and sat on the foot of the bed, in jeans and a sweater. Minuit woke and jumped down, gave an indignant mew, and wandered off down the hall.

"Is the curtain there to keep me out?" Tony asked in a tired voice. "It's okay if you want your space."

"No, no—it's because of the light from the windows in the morning," I said, gesturing toward the French doors. "I'll get drapes for them."

"Oh."

I could see him better now that my eyes were adjusting to the light. He looked tired.

"I saved you some supper," I said. "It's in the fridge."

"I ate, but thanks."

Ate what, I wondered. Junk food?

"It's good to see you," I said. "Hope you're making progress on the case."

"Yeah. Slowly, but yeah. Maybe a couple more days."

What was keeping him up so late? Talking to witnesses who worked at night? He hadn't told me much about this case. Hadn't had the chance —we'd both been busy.

He rubbed his hands over his face. "Well, I'll go sleep in the other bed. I need a shower but I'm too tired."

"You're welcome to sleep here."

He smiled wearily, leaned forward to kiss me. "Nah. I'd rather come to you clean."

He did smell a little ripe. In a not-entirely unpleasant way.

"Sleep well, then," I said.

"You too."

He stood and walked slowly down the hall to his room. I turned off the light and rolled onto my side.

Welcome home.

The staff meeting the next morning went well. Everyone was impressed with the conference table. There were eleven of us, including Nat, so I brought one of the café chairs out from my suite and sat in that. We still all fit comfortably around the table.

No one had immediate ideas about candidates for the two jobs. I invited them to come talk to me if they thought of someone later.

Dee, Rosa, and Iz all agreed to work on St.

Patrick's Day. They'd probably get some over-time, which was fine.

The first part of March was now almost completely booked up. Kris had called the people who already had reservations for the 17th, explaining the higher price and offering them the chance to re-book. Most of them had kept their reservations, expressing delight about the additional treats and the music.

I refrained from mentioning that we'd talked about grandfathering them at the regular price. Too late, since Kris had already made the calls. She was a fierce defender of our bottom line, and apparently the customers didn't mind the change, so all was well.

Kris had created some pretty little table tents adorned with shamrocks, announcing the special menu and music for that day. She was sure that we'd sell out with only this and our monthly newsletter as marketing—no need to buy advertising.

She wanted to put out the table tents right after the meeting, and I okayed it. When we adjourned, I demonstrated collapsing the capstan table, receiving a round of applause from the staff.

At my request, Dale, Ramon, and Mick helped carry chairs downstairs to Poppy and Marigold, while the others moved all but four of the remaining chairs to the walls of the upper hall. The servers had already set up the new alcoves with our lace placements, china, and silver, so they were looking less stark.

Iz brought in two more place settings each for Poppy and Marigold, to go with the conference table chairs, and I hastily put together some flower arrangements from the week's flower order, which had arrived during the staff meeting. *Much* better—we were getting close to a cozy feeling, now.

And it was time to open the front door. Rosa went to do that, welcoming happily-chattering customers into the hall. I'd have to finish the flowers for the rest of the tearoom that evening.

I headed back upstairs with Kris, who had put her table tents out in all the alcoves and in the gift shop. The upper hall looked better with the extra chairs against the wall. At my desk, I found the estimate for the new drapery dividers for the alcoves.

It was ouchy, but we needed it. The difference between doing only the new curtains and doing the whole tearoom wasn't that much. Looking at the detailed description, I realized we were replacing most of the existing drapes anyway, what with realigning the alcoves.

What the heck. Might as well go whole hog.

Hunting through the line items, I found a

price per yard for the fabric. Not bad, and it was sixty inches wide.

I wrote a note to Kris approving the purchase and asking her to buy five extra yards of the fabric if they'd sell it. I envisioned matching tea cozies in that pretty wisteria fabric. Maybe even a couple of table runners.

Okay, six yards.

Time for lunch with Gina and Angela. I went into Kris's office, but she was on the phone so I left the drapery estimate in her in box, grabbed my coat and purse, and headed downstairs.

The morning was bright, with puffy white clouds in a brilliant blue sky. Evergreens smelled vibrant and fresh after the rain, lifting my spirits at once. I drove to Piccolino and spotted Gina's car in the parking lot. Was I late? No. Head high, I went in and joined her at a table in the back corner.

"Hug!" she said, jumping up and enfolding me in a Chanel-scented embrace. "Haven't seen you in forever."

"It's been busy. Making changes at the tea-room."

"Again?"

I took a seat where I could keep an eye on the door, ordered coffee, and told Gina about the new alcoves, the new furniture (including the magical capstan table), and my move to the townhome.

"Well, no wonder you didn't make it to Hyde Park," she said.

"Yeah. Tony couldn't have gone anyway—he's up to his eyebrows in a case. We'll go soon, I promise."

"You know, you could hire a wedding planner to find you a space," she said, stirring sugar into her coffee.

Another expense? Gah.

"Why would I do that when I have you?" I said.

She shot me a look. "You don't like my ideas."

"That's not it. I'm just too picky, is all."

"Hm."

Angela appeared at the door and stood looking around the restaurant. I waved, and she came over and joined us, hanging her pink parka on the back of her chair. She met my smile with a wan little smile of her own, and submitted to a Gina hug without comment. Something was bothering her, I thought as she picked up her menu.

The waiter brought more coffee and took our orders. We all chose salads, and Gina added an order of ravioli for us to split.

"They make it in house," she told Angela. "It's really good. So's the pizza."

Angela smiled and sipped her coffee. Gina launched into a list of ideas for wedding favors: candied almonds in my bridal colors, paper napkins printed with Tony's and my names and the date, shot glasses similarly inscribed, little bags of rice for the guests to throw at me and Tony.

"No," I said. "The birds will eat it, and it's bad for them."

"Well, then, how about bird seed instead?" Gina said.

"Why do they have to throw anything?"

"It's *traditional*. I thought you liked traditions!"

Biting back a reply that I wasn't, at present, interested in the implications of that particular traditional fertility ritual, I sighed. "Fine. Bird seed."

I nixed the napkins and the shot glasses, and suggested mixed nuts instead of the designer almonds, which I was sure would be expensive. The whole idea of favors at a wedding reception was a bit off-putting for me. Shouldn't a nice meal and dancing be enough?

"How about a photo booth?" Gina suggested. "Everyone can get a souvenir picture taken with you and Tony."

"We'd be there the whole afternoon."

"Just off and on."

I shook my head, knowing Tony wouldn't

like it. Glancing at Angela, I saw she was staring at the black-and-white checkered tablecloth.

"Okay, then how about a magnet with a photo of you and Tony?" Gina said.

"What do you think, Angela?" I asked gently.

She started, looked at me, and blushed. "Sorry. What was the question?"

"A photo magnet of Ellen and Tony for a favor," Gina said. "Something the guests can keep as a memento."

Angela blinked, swallowed, and said. "Um."

Her thoughts were clearly elsewhere. To let her off the hook, I looked at Gina. "It's not quite right, I think. Kind of commercial."

"Well, they're *all* commercial, then," Gina said.

"I guess that's my point. You know I'm old-fashioned. Wouldn't the nuts and the bird seed be enough?"

"But they're not something people can take home," Gina protested.

The arrival of our salads ended the discussion for the moment. Gina shifted gears and began to talk about the menu for the reception.

"I'm leaving that up to Julio," I said, wanting to forestall yet another long discussion.

"And he's doing the cake?"

"I might ask Hanh, if he doesn't want to," I said, thinking of the design I'd seen her working on for Buddha's birthday.

The ravioli arrived and Gina busied herself dividing it onto three small plates. Angela was picking at her salad. I touched her wrist.

"Is everything okay?" I asked.

Angela looked up at me, then burst into tears.

6

Dismayed, I took Angela's hand in mine. "Do you want to go to the ladies' room?" I asked softly.

Angela shook her head, gulping for breath. I took my handkerchief—clean, fortunately—out of my purse and gave it to her. After a minute of wiping her face and a couple more sobs, she said, "Sorry."

"We could do this another time," I said.

She shook her head. "No, I'm okay. I just … I lost my job."

"Oh, honey!" Gina said.

I squeezed Angela's hand. "I'm sorry. The nursing job?"

She nodded, sniffing. "It was just part time."

"You're in school, too, though. Was it too hard to do both?"

"No. Nothing like that. It was budget cuts. They laid four of us off."

"Oh."

"I just found out this morning. Sorry," she said again.

"No, no," I said. "Totally understandable. I'd cry, too!"

She gave another couple of sniffs, wiped her nose, and started to offer me the crumpled handkerchief, then thought better of it.

"Keep it." I smiled.

She gave a watery laugh. "Thanks, Ellen."

"That's it!" Gina said.

I looked at her, confounded. Gina grinned.

"A handkerchief! Embroidered with your names and the date. That's old-fashioned, right?"

I drew a breath, glancing at Angela. She was wiping her eyes. To give her some space to recover, I turned to Gina. "Uh. Well, yes."

"It'll be *perfect!*" Gina said.

"Brilliant!" Actually I wasn't sure about it, but it didn't bother me nearly as much as the photo magnet idea.

Angela had recovered enough to start actually eating her salad. Gina chattered away about the handkerchiefs, and then the reception, which gave Angela more room to get her balance back. I listened and watched, and ate my lunch, wondering how best to help both of them.

Apparently Gina's feelings were a little hurt by my nixing many of her ideas. But she had so *many* ideas. She was trying to please me, I knew. It was just that her notions of fun and mine were not exactly the same.

Angela was more of a concern. Losing the income, even from a part-time job, was probably painful for her. She caught me watching her, and gave me a wry smile.

Gina headed off the the restroom, and I took the opportunity to offer Angela some support. "I'm so sorry about your job. How can I help?"

She sighed. "It's fine. It was kind of a pain anyway, trying to schedule hours around my classes. I'll find something else. I can always get a fast food job."

"Ugh. You deserve better than that."

She shrugged. "That's what I did before I started studying nursing."

I watched her eat a bite of ravioli. "Did you *like* the nursing job?"

"It was a job."

"But was it rewarding?"

"The money was nice." A flicker of unhappiness crossed her face. She had bills to pay, of course.

I tilted my head, watching her. An idea was beginning to tickle.

"Are you busy after lunch?" I asked.

Another sigh. "I was supposed to work this afternoon. So, no. I'm not busy."

Gina was returning. "Could you come to the tearoom for a while?" I said.

Angela looked at me in surprise. "Okay."

Gina settled in her chair, smiling. She wanted dessert, so we ordered a piece of Italian wedding cake and a chocolate mousse and split them three ways while we discussed how to present the mixed nuts attractively. I was for just serving them in a cup, but Gina wanted to make them another keepsake by putting them in a pretty box with Tony's and my names on it (again). I pointed out there was no need to duplicate what would be on the handkerchiefs.

"Well, just your initials, then," Gina said.

"But printing is expensive."

"It's included when you order the nuts."

"I was thinking Julio could make the nuts, and I could package them. They'll be fresher, and I'm sure they'd be better than anything we could order. Kris can find me some nice little paper boxes for them. How about turquoise and violet?"

Gina thought about it, then nodded. "That would be pretty."

"I-I could calligraph your initials on them, if you like," Angela offered.

"Oh, how lovely!" I said, smiling.

"Yes!" Gina said. "And we can help you fill the boxes. We'll make it a party! We'll do up the bird seed in little individual bags, too."

"Sounds like fun," I said.

"So we'll have the handkerchiefs, the nuts—one more favor would be good," Gina said.

"There's the bird seed," I reminded her.

"That doesn't count. They're going to throw it at you."

"A printed menu, then?" That would be something that could have the date on it, maybe that would please her.

"Hm," Gina said.

"A printed menu and a place card with their name on it?" I offered.

"Oh, that's nice. And 'Ellen and Tony's Wedding' at the bottom," Gina said, making a note on her pad.

"Fine." I could tolerate that, and it wouldn't be expensive. We could print menus and place cards at the tearoom.

"What if people have trouble finding their places at the tables, though?" Gina said. "If there are a lot of guests, it could be a problem."

"We can let them pick up their place cards on the way in and choose their own seats," I said.

She nodded. "That works."

By this time we'd polished off the desserts. Gina insisted on picking up the tab, hugged me and Angela, and took off for her office. I walked out to the parking lot with Angela.

She was looking better. Maybe just talking about losing the job had helped. That, and the chocolate.

"Come on by the tearoom. You can park in the back with me," I told her.

She smiled bravely. "Okay."

We arrived at about two o'clock, and went in the back door. The tearoom was calm; customers had their tea and were enjoying it while the servers prepared for the next seating. Gentle piano music—a nocturne—enhanced the peaceful mood. I peeked into the dining parlor. No customers, so I showed Angela the new alcoves, then led her up front to the gift shop.

No customers in there, either. A quiet murmur of voices from Dahlia and Violet.

"You've changed this, too," Angela said.

"Yes. More room for merchandise, and the alcoves are less crowded."

She picked up a teacup decorated with roses from the china display, turning it around in her hands. "So pretty. *Abuela* would like this."

I smiled. "Maybe you could get it for her."

She glanced at the tag and carefully set it down. "Maybe when I get another job."

"I wanted to talk to you about that. I need to hire a manager for this gift shop. Would you be interested?"

Angela froze and looked up at me, astonished.

"It isn't nursing, but we could work with you on the hours," I added, recklessly throwing our plan for a full-time manager out the window.

She blushed deeply. "You don't have to make up a job for me."

"I'm not, I swear. We're about to advertise it in the paper, but you could save us the trouble if you're interested. Why don't we go upstairs and have a cup of tea and discuss it?"

She agreed, looking a little dazed as we went upstairs. I poured tea for us from the samovar (Assam, thankfully, not Lapsang Souchong) and invited her to join me by the front windows. She settled into an armchair with a sigh.

"It's so nice here," she said.

I smiled. "That's the idea. When I created the tearoom, I wanted a place where people would feel comfortable. Maybe you'd like to be here every day?"

She swallowed. "I don't have any experience running a shop."

"We can teach you. It isn't rocket science. You'd be in charge of picking out merchandise, ordering it, and helping customers when you're here."

"I can't do full time, though. I have school."

"We can cover the gift shop when you're not here. We cover it all the time, now, but it's getting to be too much work for us. I need someone to be in charge of it."

She gave me an earnest, searching look. Wanting to be sure this wasn't a handout.

"I know it's not your chosen career," I said. "When you need to move on, it'll be fine."

She ducked her head, laughing softly. "I'm afraid I won't want to move on. This would be so much nicer than working at the hospital."

"Well, you can cross that bridge when you come to it," I said gently.

She pressed her lips together, then looked up at me. "Okay." She nodded. "Yes, I'd like to try it. Thank you, Ellen."

"Thank *you,*" I said. "I'd much rather hire a friend than a stranger."

I told her the starting pay we were offering, which made her eyes go wide. "You'll get an employee discount on merchandise, too—and on tea, of course," I said, standing. I beckoned Angela to come with me and turned her over to Kris, who shot a questioning glance at me when I mentioned the job would be part-time, then welcomed Angela with a smile.

While they sorted out the details—forms, hours, and so on—I refilled my teacup and went to my desk. I'd have to accelerate the timing on moving out of this office, I realized. Gazing around at the furniture, I pictured it in my old bedroom. Pretty much the same arrangement, except mirror image, with the window on my right. I'd have a little less room, because the two sides of the house were not exactly symmetrical, but I'd still have the rest of my suite.

I sent Kris a private message: "Go ahead and order your new desk."

Sitting back with my teacup in hand, I smiled.

I think I did a good thing.

That evening after the tearoom had closed, I was downstairs arranging flowers when I got a text from Phillips: two photos of a little round, misshapen, black lump sitting on a metal table.

> You were right. It's a pistol ball. Got a little flattened going into the wall, but I think I can still pull some ballistics off it.

Exciting! I texted back my thanks and an enthusiastic thumbs-up for ballistics. He reminded me that we'd need ballistics from a weapon to compare it to.

I had exactly the weapon in mind. I'd call Mr. Hidalgo in the morning. Rather than texting the details, I called Phillips and explained my speculation to him.

"Okay," Phillips said. "I can set up a time to fire the pistol at a shooting range, but I don't have the tools to make pistol balls. You might ask the history museum."

"Actually I think I know someone who can help with that, a Civil War reenactor. I'll make some calls and get back to you."

"Ah, great. Talk to you later, then."

Humming, I added baby's breath to a teapot vase of roses and lilies. My phone buzzed with another text and I glanced at it, wondering what else Phillips would say.

> Where are you?

Tony! I put down the flowers and grabbed my phone.

> At the tearoom,
> finishing up some stuff.
> Are you at the house?

> Yeah. Starving. Want to eat
> out?

> Okay. How about
> Tomasita's?

Sure.

Come down to the
tearoom and I'll drive.

I suggested Tomasita's because it was New Mexican and relatively close, and we'd probably be able to get a table quickly. Also, they made good margaritas.

I'd do the rest of the flowers in the morning. I finished the teapot vase and put it in Rose, stuffed the other flowers in the walk-in fridge, cleaned up my mess and hurried upstairs for my coat and purse. By the time I got back downstairs, Tony's headlight was shining into the hall through the lights around the back door. He joined me as I locked up, opening his arms wide for a hug.

"Missed you," I said snuggling close. His leather jacket was cold.

He kissed my temple, which was what he could reach. "Let's go."

The drive was short, and there was only one party ahead of us, so we were soon sipping margaritas while we awaited our food. This was significant; Tony probably wouldn't be having a strong drink if he intended to go back to work.

"How's the case going?" I asked.

"It's done. All but the paperwork."

"Wonderful! Congratulations."

He nodded, and took a long pull at his glass. Offered no elaboration. Maybe I didn't want to know the details.

He looked tired, and a little sad. Becoming aware of my gaze, he gave me a half-hearted smile. "Sorry I haven't been home much."

I smiled back. "Well, I haven't either. The weekend was busy."

"You got moved all right."

"Yes. I still need to move my office across the hall."

Our dinners arrived: enchiladas for Tony, *rellenos* for me. I took a bite, savoring the warmth and the spice. Just right for a cold night. I ate half of the first *relleno*, then took a breather.

"Have you talked to Angela lately?" I asked.

Tony shook his head, mouth full. I sipped my margarita.

"She lost her job this morning."

"Crap!" Tony said. He pulled out his phone.

"She was having lunch with Gina and me, and she told us. As it happens, we've been looking for someone to run the tearoom's gift shop, so I offered the position to her. She's going to try it."

He stared at me, blinking as he took that in. "You didn't have to—"

"She's perfect, really. She likes pretty things, she's creative, and she has a good eye. I'm sure she'll be great."

Tony put his phone down, frowning slightly.

"I'm so happy to have someone I know for this, and not a stranger," I added.

He looked down at his plate and pushed some beans around with his fork, reminding me strongly of his sister. Maybe he didn't like me hiring Angela? Well, tough.

He ate a couple of bites in silence. I did the same.

Was it pride, I wondered? Did he dislike the idea that Angela would be under my authority? I was tempted to assure him that I'd be good to her, but that might not help. He was touchy sometimes, and apparently this was such a time.

More margarita. I stifled a sigh and drank. It was already going to my head, despite the food.

Tony finished chewing a bite and swallowed. "It's nice of you to give her a job."

"Well, she's family. You help your family out when you can."

He shot me a glance, then took a swig of margarita.

"Lucky we had the opening," I added. "We were about to put an ad in the paper."

We didn't talk about it any more. We didn't talk much at all, in fact. Tony was plainly tired, and I was wary of pushing his emotional buttons. We decided against dessert, paid the bill and returned to the tearoom, where Tony got on his bike and followed me up to the townhome.

The porch light gleamed a warm welcome. There was just enough room in the garage for Tony to pull in beside my car, if I kept close to the wall. We went in the house and Minuit came running, crying at me.

"I take it you didn't feed her," I said, picking her up.

"I don't know how."

"Oh, okay. I'll show you."

He headed off down the hall, toward the guest bathroom.

"Another time," I added, putting the kitten down. She ghosted about my feet as I dished up her supper. Leaving her munching, I headed for the master bedroom, shedding my coat. I paused to peek into Tony's room, where he was taking off his boots.

"Hot tub?" I said.

"Yeah. Be right there."

Sometimes a hot bath is just the right cure for a weary mind and body. Add some bubble jets and a glass of brandy—thank you Tony (and no I didn't care that it was my cooking brandy)—and you pretty much have to relax.

"We're out of whiskey," Tony said as he handed me a glass before climbing in.

"Yes, I drank the last little bit. Sorry."

"I drank a lot more of it than you did."

Not the time to comment about that. I sipped the brandy and rolled it around on my tongue.

"Owen drank some, too," Tony said, settling in beside me.

"He did?"

"Yeah. He dropped by a couple of times."

"Oh."

He took a sip of brandy. "He's all right."

High praise, coming from Tony. Owen must have said the right things.

The tipsiness was returning. I leaned my head back and closed my eyes. A moment later, I felt a touch on my thigh underwater.

Some kinds of communication are less complicated. I put my glass in a cup holder and let worries about Angela and moving and all the rest drift away on the night.

Welcome home.

Wednesday morning I left Tony sleeping while I filled my car with empty boxes and took them to the tearoom so I could clear out my desk and credenza. I carried the boxes upstairs, went down to the kitchen to finish arranging the fresh flowers, then returned to my office and began loading boxes with files.

For now, Angela would be working Tuesdays, Wednesdays, Fridays and Saturdays, about twenty-four hours a week. She had classes on Thursday, so she would start work on Friday. Kris's desk set was expected Thursday; it would need to be assembled, but she assured me she could handle that. I had to get my office moved by Thursday afternoon.

Kris came in and handed me a lavender message slip. "Can I have a couple of boxes?"

"Sure," I said, reading the message. It was from the Bird Woman:

> *Found a place for your wedding.*
> *Silly Samba. Call me.*

"Silly Samba?"

"I have no idea," Kris said. "I just pulled it off the voicemail."

Urgh. Visions of a dance hall complete with mirror ball arose in my mind. No. Just, no. I dropped the message in my in box. I'd deal with it later.

There were other phone calls to make, and I made them. Mr. Hidalgo was open to having his ancestor's pistol fired in a ballistics test. Could he come and watch? Of course.

Mr. Quentin was extremely interested in the project. "You can order cartridges for the pistol online," he told me. "You'll need percussion caps, too. I will send you a link."

"Thank you! So you don't cast your own balls?"

"Actually I do, but the ones you can order will be fine for the purposes of a ballistics test. Might I come and observe?"

"Of course," I said, compounding my rash promise to bring an audience to the test. I hoped Phillips wouldn't mind.

The morning was mostly gone, and I hadn't even gone downstairs to check on the tearoom. I did so, and found the gift shop's displays looking a little sparse. We were almost fully booked that day, and Dale and Rosa had their hands full. I restocked the tables, making an executive decision to break into the "Irish stuff" to fill in where all the Valentine's stuff had sold.

Well, there were only three more business days of February left. I went ahead and removed the pink decorations from the seasonal table and set it up with shamrocks and lace. The select pieces of Belleek china went in the middle, on top of some boxes draped in lace over a white cloth, with a little sign advising shoppers to ask for help before handling them. Less expensive china (also with shamrocks), and some cute mugs with rainbows, went on the more accessible lower level. No pots of gold.

As I finished the display with a basket of lace

and linens, two customers came in after their tea and immediately bought some.

We might need to order extra Irish stuff. I'd have to let Kris know… or let Angela know.

Smiling, I tidied up the boxes I'd broken into, then went to the kitchen to see how things were going there. Hanh and Julio were both up to their elbows in work. I abandoned my faint hope that there would be more Rubens, and returned upstairs to see if Kris wanted to share some takeout.

We got Indian food and ate it together at the capstan table. Both of our offices were a mess, with half-filled boxes sitting around. I was really getting tired of moving, but it would be over soon. I'd keep telling myself that.

After lunch, Kris helped me carry my chaise longue into my new office. I took the stained glass standing lamp as well, and arranged them together on the north wall, then brought my print of Monet's water lilies in and hung it above the chaise.

The wardrobe would stay by the window on the south wall, and would hold extra office supplies and maybe a nice dress or two for emergencies. The room would look more balanced when I got my desk and the credenza in there.

I turned the standing lamp on to make sure

the bulb was still working, and it cast a warm glow of jeweled light into the room. That was lovely.

Leaving it on, I went back to packing, resisting the temptation to curl up on the chaise with a book. By late afternoon I had my credenza and desk emptied out except for my computer and the office phone. Kris offered to move the phone for me the next morning. She was ready to take the day's receipts to the bank, so we said goodnight and she left.

Turning to my phone, I texted Tony a request for help moving the desk and credenza. He came back surprisingly fast:

> Sorry, can't. Working late.
> Helping Zeke with a new
> case.

Here we go again. Sighing, I powered down my computer, unhooked all the cabling spaghetti, and moved it to the café table in my suite. In case I'd need to use it before I got the desk moved I cabled it up again, and sent a test page to the Bluetooth printer in Kris's office to make sure it could still connect.

It was well past six before I pulled on my coat, locked up my suite after turning off the standing lamp, and went downstairs. Everyone else had left, even Mick. I stood in the hall at the foot of the stairs, just listening to the silence for a moment.

So many changes, and we still hadn't been open for quite a year. I felt tired, but I still needed to get the desk and credenza moved. It would be better to do it when the tearoom was closed, in case we made a lot of noise.

Well, I'd eat something first, and then maybe beg Owen for assistance.

I drove home, made myself some eggs and toast, then called Owen. Got voicemail. Left a message, and was considering the hot tub when my phone rang: Owen, calling back.

"Hey, Ellen! Sorry, we were in the middle of a song."

"Oh, if you're busy—"

"Dale and I are rehearsing for St. Patrick's Day. Want to come over? We're at the studio."

He gave me the address, which was three doors down from my house. I walked over and rang the doorbell. Owen answered it, looking rather breathtaking in a white silk shirt with his hair loose over his shoulders.

"Hi, neighbor! Come on in!"

He opened the door to a hall filled with light, very different from his and Julio's house, where the light was subdued and cozy. Here it was brilliant, illuminating white walls covered with framed photographs: Owen's work, for I recognized one or two. I wanted to study them, but Owen was headed for the living room, so I followed.

Like his other townhomes, this one had large picture windows with a spectacular view of Santa Fe. The room was filled with light, music stands, sound equipment, a desk covered in electronic equipment and a big flatscreen monitor, a magnificent concert grand piano, and the golden baroque glory of a concert harp. Dale grinned at me from a chair behind a music stand, an Irish flute in his hands.

"Hi, Ellen!"

"Hi," I said, slightly stunned by it all.

"All moved in?" Owen said.

"Yes. Well, no, not quite—I was hoping to impose on you for some help moving my office furniture at the tearoom."

"Oh, sure. Sunday again?"

"Are you free tomorrow morning? I'll shower you with gifts in appreciation."

"I can help," Dale offered.

"Mm—I think I'll need you in the tearoom. We're booked up again."

"Well, we'll make it happen, one way or another," Owen promised. "Have a seat and listen to this."

He sat at the harp and leaned it back against

his shoulder. Dale was in the only other chair, so I went to the piano—the Steinway—and sat on the bench. A glance passed between them, and Dale raised his flute to his lips.

The sound was deeper than I expected, and a little raw. The melody rose up, lilting, sad. It sounded vaguely familiar—I must have heard it before, but I couldn't place it.

Dale played the whole verse alone, then on the next time through Owen came in softly with just the tonic on a low string, supporting the melody but leaving the flute in command. After the second time through, Dale lowered the flute and sang to the accompaniment of gentle chords from the harp.

> *My young love said to me,*
> *My mother won't mind*
> *And my father won't slight you*
> *For your lack of kine.*
> *And she stepped away from me*
> *And this she did say:*
> *It will not be long, love,*
> *'Til our wedding day.*

Oh. A wedding song. My mind went to Tony, of course. Owen filled in more strongly with the harp as Dale sang on.

She stepped away from me
And she moved through the fair
And fondly I watched her
Move here and move there.
Then she made her way homeward,
With one star awake,
As the swan in the evening
Moved over the lake.

Beautiful lyrics. I'd relaxed, and now Owen joined in, adding an exquisite vocal harmony and a subtle increase of energy.

The people were saying,
No two e'er were wed
But one had a sorrow
That never was said.
And I smiled as she passed
With her goods and her gear,
And that was the last
That I saw of my dear.

My throat tightened with sudden sadness and a trace of alarm. Superstition made me not want to hear more. Foolish, of course. This wasn't me and Tony, it was just a sad old Irish ballad, one of many.

Dale lifted the flute and they played through one verse instrumentally. It gave me a moment to recover my balance, and to think about the story so far. Then the harp dropped back to near silence, silvery high notes in *tremulo,* and Dale sang alone again.

> *Last night she came to me,*
> *My dead love came in.*
> *So softly she came*
> *That her feet made no din.*
> *And she laid her hand on me,*
> *And this she did say:*
> *It will not be long, love,*
> *'Til our wedding day.*

Dale put the flute to his lips and played the last line over again while Owen's hands moved lower on the harp, finishing with a single low string on the tonic. I held still while the note hovered and faded. In the following silence, I swallowed.

Owen looked at me, smiling. "What do you think?"

"It's lovely," I said. "So sad. I know I've heard it before, but I never payed attention to the lyrics."

"Oh, yeah, a lot of people have covered it. Sinead O'Connor, Loreena McKennitt. But usually solo. We added the harmony. Is it too much?"

"It's gorgeous."

Owen smiled. "I thought Captain Dusenberry

might like it. Does he listen to the music in the tearoom?"

"I'm sure he does. He even plays occasionally."

"What—he plays music?" Owen's eyes lit with interest.

"On the piano." I laid a hand on the Steinway. "May I?"

"Sure!"

I opened the keyboard cover and turned on the bench to face it. "He plays this," I said, and gently played the opening of "Contessa Perdono" as the captain had played it a few nights ago.

Contessa perdono,
perdono, perdono

The piano's action was delicious, the sound rich and soft. Suddenly Dale's flute picked up the Contessa's melody, sending a chill up my spine. Owen added chords softly in the background, and I caught my breath. They both knew the piece!

The flute carried on with the soprano's line, the Contessa's declaration that she was kinder, she would say yes. As the song continued I softly picked out one of the chorus's lines on the piano, afraid of bungling and ruining the harmony, while Owen filled in the chords on the harp.

I did not bungle. I added low chords. It was exquisite, a magical moment of spontaneous music.

"Oh, yeah," Owen breathed after we stopped at the end of the song.

Dale chuckled softly. "That was great."

"Too bad it's not Irish," Owen said. "It would sound great in the tearoom. We could play it for the captain, maybe, when we come to rehearse."

I smiled softly. "He'd probably like that."

Owen met my gaze, returning the smile. "Now you have to join our band."

Feeling shy suddenly, I looked at Dale. "I didn't know you knew Mozart."

"He studied at a conservatory—didn't he tell you?" Owen said.

I shook my head.

Dale shrugged. "I dropped out, so..."

"I've been telling him he should go back," Owen said.

My staff was so multi-talented. Julio with his painting; Ramon, Dee, and now Dale with music; and of course Vi had been musically gifted as well.

Vi. My mind conjured her up as Mozart's Contessa: tall and beautiful, regal despite the maid's clothing she had donned to unmask the Count's infidelity. I could almost hear her singing her forgiveness.

I brushed away a tear.

"Don't worry," Dale said. "I'm not going back. I hated Cleveland."

"It isn't that," I said, smiling as I shook my head. "It's just … memories." I cleared my throat and pulled myself together. "Well, I'll let you finish your rehearsal—"

"We're done," Owen said, easing the harp to a standing position. "We'll add 'She Moved Through the Fair' to the playlist. We've got it all now. I'll send you the final list."

Dale gathered up several other flutes and put them all into a quilted fabric case—black with a silvery-gray paisley pattern. "We could go move that furniture now, if you like," he said, looking at me.

"Yes," Owen said. "Let's do that."

I closed the Steinway's keyboard lid. "If it isn't too late, that would be wonderful."

"How much furniture?"

"My desk and a credenza."

"No problem."

Owen drove us to the tearoom in his Mercedes, which was luxuriously comfortable. The leather seats were heated, I realized as my tired back was gently warmed.

"Nice ride," Dale said.

"Thanks. Might get rid of it, though. I'm

thinking about getting an electric car."

Dale nodded. "That would be cool."

Whew. Cutting edge, but Owen could afford it.

And here he was, about to move furniture for me, when he had no need to do so. He could have paid someone to do it. Well, so could I— but that would create a delay, and Dale and Owen were willing to do it now. Their kindness humbled me.

They wouldn't let me help, other than showing them where I wanted things. I pulled my desk chair and guest chairs out into the hall, and moved the samovar table out of the way. They carried the credenza across first, then the empty desk. The whole thing took less than ten minutes.

"Thank you so much!" I said. "I owe you … something amazing."

Owen grinned. "Come play music with us," he said.

"I'd love to."

I would also give them each a gift, I decided as Owen drove us back to his studio, where Dale's car was parked. They were putting a lot of time into creating the music for St. Patrick's day, time that I wasn't paying them for. Gift cards from Ten Thousand Waves would be good.

We said goodnight and I walked home. It had

been a magical evening, but it was time to rest. I went in the front door. Minuit came running to greet me, and I decided I could use some cuddle time with her. I didn't have a cuddle-worthy chair at the house, but Tony's armchair would do.

He had picked up his room, I noticed as I settled in with the kitten in my lap. The scattered laundry was gone, and the pile of mail on the coffee table was smaller and tidily stacked.

A small, warm, purring bundle of fur in my lap was even better than heated leather seats. I gave a contented sigh, thinking back to the beautiful music Owen and Dale had made in the studio, and that I'd had the honor of making with them. Their talent greatly exceeded mine, but I could practice. I was definitely rusty. I hadn't played much since the tearoom had opened.

That realization surprised me. Music had always been a big part of my life, but the last year had been so busy I hadn't had time. Music had been made at the tearoom, but not by me.

Well, maybe it was time to get back to it. Playing, and singing, had always lifted my heart. I'd do it, I promised myself, closing my eyes and remembering the joy of the spontaneous Mozart.

We were on the gazebo in Santa Fe's Plaza, play-ing "Contessa Perdono." The Spanish Market was in full swing, and I could see Captain Dusenberry threading his way through the crowd, looking for someone—Maria, I thought. I glimpsed a female form in white on the other side of the plaza, but I couldn't tell if it was Maria or Vi, and the captain was too far away to hear me if I called out, and anyway I was busy singing "She Moved Through the Fair." I didn't know the words, so I was making them up, worried that I'd screw it up. As the song came to an end, Phillips stepped up onto the stage with a Colt Navy Pistol in his hand and protective earmuffs on his head. I tried to catch his eye and warn him not to fire, but he didn't notice me. He aimed the barrel skyward and pulled the trigger, and there was a loud *bang*.

7

I WOKE, STARTLED. Minuit jumped off my lap and scuttled out of the room. I stood and went out into the hall, rubbing my eyes. Tony was in the kitchen, taking off his jacket.

"Hi," I said, joining him.

"Sorry the door slammed." He hung the jacket on a chair and folded me into his arms. "And sorry I missed dinner. Still want to move furniture?"

"Owen and Dale did it for me."

He leaned back, looking surprised.

"They were rehearsing music for St. Patrick's Day, and I went over to listen."

Tony frowned. "Need more data."

I explained in the hot tub. We'd both been so busy that I hadn't told him about St. Patrick's or why I was moving my office.

"It's so Kris can have my old office, and Angela can have hers," I said, gazing up at the stars in the cold night sky.

"You're giving Ange an office?" Tony said.

"She'll need it. It's right next to the store-room where we keep extra merchandise, and she'll be in charge of that."

"Um. Thank you for doing this. Giving her a job." He sounded less hesitant this time.

"I'm very happy to do it," I told him.

"She's really excited about it. I talked to her."

"Good."

I slid into his lap, wanting human cuddles now instead of kitty cuddles. It was cold, so we soon went inside and curled up together in bed. I drifted to sleep with the memory of Owen's harp ringing in my head.

Angela fit into the tearoom staff like a rose into a bouquet. It took a little nudging to get her to unleash her creativity in the gift shop, but within a week she was sealing each takeout box with shamrock stickers and making shamrocks for little signs out of paper doilies. She surprised me with excellent calligraphy, though more modern in style than mine. The gift shop began to look even more charming and posh.

The servers were suddenly more relaxed with the burden of minding the shop largely removed. Nat was happy to step back from helping out, and Kris was happier too. She had more space, physically as well as temporally, and was able to focus better on her administrative tasks.

Her new office looked far more impressive than mine, with her Goth black desk, file cabinet, credenza, and a matching printer stand; her print of "Drowned Ophelia" hanging where my water lilies had been; and Gabriel's painting "Calculation" on the wall behind her desk. Woe to the sales rep who tried to cajole her in that room.

Angela began popping in before or after classes on her off days just to check on the shop and tend the displays, and I had to scold her to log her time for those visits. She was having a blast.

I had given her a list of our suppliers, and when she brought me her merchandise choices for approval, I learned that she had discovered several new sources and some really lovely items that I wouldn't have thought of.

Meanwhile I struggled to finish moving into my new office and my new home, while being pelted alternately by Gina's ideas about the wedding and messages from the Bird Woman insisting I come and look at Silly Samba. I ignored most of them, and put off talking about it when I couldn't ignore. There were bigger tasks before me: I still had to find more furniture for the new alcoves, and some furniture for my living room, and we needed to hire that extra server. No one on the staff had come up with a candidate, other than Dale's half-hearted suggestion that Cherie Legrand might be interested.

Cherie, though, had issues to work through, and I suspected she had enough money that she didn't need an entry-level job. Dale confirmed this, adding that what she'd get out of it was structure and interaction with people who were more emotionally healthy than she. I wished her well, but I wasn't ready to offer her a job as therapy. The memory of her weeping and bleeding in the Rose alcove after the disastrous masquerade was too vivid.

So we resorted to advertising the job, and Kris and I sifted through the subsequent deluge of applicants, choosing half a dozen to interview. All six looked promising, and to my surprise I had met one of them before: Nicholas, one of the Bird Woman's elf assistants from her Christmas tea for the women from Esperanza.

His chestnut hair was nearly as long as Owen's, I recalled, but on the day he came to interview he had it confined in a man-bun. His button-down shirt, tie, and formal slacks were a world apart from the medieval tunic and holly crown I'd first seen him in. He was a little nervous, but lit the room with a beautiful smile as he came in, and I had a feeling I'd found my new server.

"Hi, Nicholas," I said, inviting him to sit in one of my guest chairs. "Nice to see you again."

"Thanks for considering me," he said, gracefully folding his tall, slender form into the chair. "I had a great time doing Auntie Ginny's Christmas thing, so when I saw the job listing I had to put my name in."

"Auntie Ginny?"

"Well, she's my mom's aunt, actually, but that's what we call her."

Ah. The Bird Woman.

Nicholas gave good answers to all of my questions. The only issue was that he was finishing his senior year in high school and would have limited availability until he graduated in May.

"Would you be able to work Saturdays until then?" I asked.

He nodded. "And I can work around my classes. School gets out at three. Would that help?" he asked, anxious hope in his voice.

"I think so. If you could work three-thirty to six-thirty on Tuesday through Friday, and eight hours on Saturday, that would give you twenty hours a week. Then in summer we could expand your hours."

He smiled, looking relieved. But was he only looking for a summer job? It would be better for us to hire someone who'd stick around for a while.

"What are your college plans?" I asked.

"UNM," he said instantly. "Auntie Ginny offered to pay for me to go out of state, but I want to stay home."

"Would you want to keep working when you start classes in the fall?"

"Yeah, for sure," he said, and flashed a smile. "I want to get my own apartment."

"All right. Thank you. We'll be in touch."

We stood and shook hands, and Nicholas left. I liked him better than the two other perfectly acceptable candidates I'd already interviewed. As it turned out, I liked him better than the remaining three as well. Kris had met each of them when they came in to interview, and when we sat down together to go over their resumés, I asked her which ones had given her the best impression.

"Nicholas Howell," she said at once.

"Why?"

"He wants it the most. And he's naturally graceful."

Neither of those had been on his resumé. Said resumé was actually pretty scant, consisting of a part-time job at the city library and a work-study job in the high school theater department.

Kris and I talked over all the candidates, just to be thorough, but I was leaning more and more toward Nicholas. In the end, we offered him the job, and he joyfully accepted. Kris put him through all the paperwork, and when he started work, I handed him over to Dale for training.

Nat accompanied me on a trip to Albuquerque to shop for furniture. Tony had said he didn't care what the living room stuff looked like as long as it was comfortable. Though that gave me carte blanche to fill the room with frou-frou, I actually wanted something more like what Owen and Julio had—understated, classic, peaceful furnishings that would make for relaxing evenings and not compete with the magnificent view of Santa Fe.

I ended up choosing a sofa set in a quiet sage with a matching armchair, and an oak coffee table. Four of the dining room chairs, plus a few odds and ends from my storage shed, filled in the gaps for now, and Tony and I finally had a place to hang out in comfort and entertain guests.

Our first guests were Nat and Manny. On a Saturday evening I made lemon-roasted chicken, rice pilaf, and a big salad, with a caramel cake for dessert. I loved cake, and hadn't been able to bake a full-sized one while living in the tearoom unless I went downstairs and used the industrial oven. I was reveling in my new, very own full-sized oven.

When we were all stuffed silly, we retired to the living room with glasses of whiskey. Tony built a fire in the kiva fireplace, and the lights of Santa Fe twinkled beautifully outside the window.

"That view is stunning," Nat said, leaning back and swirling the single ice cube in her glass.

"Yes, I love it," I said. "We're so lucky."

"How's the wedding planning going?"

Agh. *Et tu,* Nat?

I took a swig of whiskey. "Still looking for a venue."

"Hm. Better decide, before they all book up."

"I know, I know. Gina's been nagging me. Tony, let's go look at Hyde Park tomorrow."

"Okay," he said, without noticeable enthusiasm.

"Oh, that's a pretty place! May we come along?" Nat said.

"Sure. We can make it a picnic. It's supposed to be sunny."

Nat and I collaborated on the picnic, and we all went in Nat's car. I made chicken salad from the leftover chicken and brought the rest of the caramel cake, while Nat brought her wonderful homemade green chile cheese bread and some pickles.

Hyde State Park was a wilderness area centered around an historic lodge that was right by the road a mile or so beyond Ten Thousand Waves. There were some camping areas and hiking trails, but it was the lodge and its grounds we were interested in. Tall ponderosas surrounded the open area around the building, and the white trunks of aspens—bare at this season— were scattered among them. In September the aspen leaves might be beginning to go golden, which would be pretty.

The lodge was a huge, old, asymmetrical stone structure with a large *portal* on the west side, three fireplaces, and a shed roof. We climbed the (many) stone steps up to the building. The *portal* was shady and cold, so we went around to the back where there was a big patio.

There were no picnic tables nearby, so we used a round thingie made of stacked flagstone at the focus of the patio. It looked like an oversized well, and from photos I'd seen on the website it was where wedding ceremonies were usually staged, with the wedding party standing in front of the well-thing and guests seated on folding chairs on the patio.

The well-thing was about ten feet in diameter, with a smaller well in the middle that was probably a firepit. The curved walls had *bancos* on the inside for sitting around the fire. We spread our picnic out along the shady side *banco* and filled our paper plates, then sat on the sunnier *banco* to eat. It was cool but the sun was warm, and with sweaters on we were perfectly comfortable.

I ate a slice of pickle. It was fresh, crunchy, and salty-sour. "Mm! Oh, those are fabulous! You made them?"

"This morning," Nat said. "They're super easy. You just slice them up, put them in a jar, add vinegar and spices, then shake it and stick it in the fridge."

"Oh, man. I'm going to have to do that." I helped myself to a small pile of the pickles, putting it on my paper plate.

A couple of cars drove by on their way up the mountain. Was there still skiing, I wondered? It was getting late in the season, but there was snow on the peaks of the *Sangre de Cristos*.

When we'd eaten enough and the cake was all gone, we packed up the remains of our picnic and went to peer through the windows at the inside of the lodge. The floors were flagstone— might be a little rough for dancing. Round tables and folding chairs were stacked at one end of the main hall. I couldn't see into the small room that was the only available food prep space, though I thought it must be behind a door at the middle of the hall. Gina was right, Julio wouldn't like it.

While my vision was for an outdoor wedding, I didn't love the big flat patio here, nor the well-thing. September would be warm and the patio might turn into an anvil of heat, with no shade.

Tony and I walked around it once more while Nat and Manny took the picnic things back to Nat's car. We stood in front of the well-thing, and I tried to imagine taking our vows here.

A pickup roared by on the road. I frowned at it.

"Gonna be traffic," Tony said, reading my thoughts. "More traffic, in September."

"Yeah," I said. "I think this isn't the place."

"Glad to hear it."

I met his gaze. "Why?"

He sighed. "Weddings are chaotic. I worked a case on a stabbing that happened at a wedding here."

"Oh, no! Why didn't you tell me?"

"Because if you loved this place, it wouldn't matter."

"But I want *you* to be happy too, at the wedding."

He slid his arms around my waist. "I'll be happy wherever you want to get married."

I chuckled. "Even at Silly Samba?"

"Huh?"

"Nothing. The Bird Woman is trying to get me to look at a place."

"Oh."

"Maybe I'll have to resort to it."

His mouth quirked in a smile. "I can't dance the samba."

"We could take lessons."

"Right. In our spare time."

"Point taken." I sighed. "Okay, not Hyde Park. I'll go back to my B-list."

Which was on my computer at the tearoom. Well, it was Sunday—theoretically my day off. I didn't need to be in my office. I could leave it until tomorrow.

Monday was March 14th, and Owen and Dale would be coming in to rehearse for Thursday. I went in early at 7:30, planning to get caught up on everything so I could listen to the rehearsal. The sun was up, and while the air was still cool it had not frozen overnight, and the morning felt spring-like.

Julio and Hanh were at the tearoom before me, making soda bread and scones for the week. Julio's salsa music wafted softly through the kitchen as I came in to say hello—he kept it quieter these days out of deference to Hanh—and the smell of his coffee made me yearn for some, but I went upstairs instead and fired up the samovar for tea. It was the warmth of a beverage I wanted, not coffee specifically, and I didn't want to get that cranked up on caffeine.

I'd been sleeping better since I'd moved to the townhome. Possibly the kitchen crew's early presence in the house had troubled my sleep even though they were usually quiet, or perhaps being so close to my office had kept me thinking about work. Or, you know, sleeping with Tony might have something to do with it. Whatever the reason, I was feeling more rested and less under pressure since the move.

Alone upstairs (Kris would be in for a half-day in the afternoon), I pulled out my to-do list from Saturday, crossed off everything that had been done, and copied over the things that hadn't to a fresh page, adding more to-dos from my messages and writing WEDDING at the top in block letters, underlined. Tearoom stuff first, though.

Then the ballistics test, which was proving complicated to arrange. Phillips was busy a lot, but was willing to book space for us at a shooting range (something I knew nothing about) on a Saturday.

I was in the midst of a flurry of messages

trying to find a Saturday that would work for all of us: me, Phillips, Mr. Hidalgo, and Mr. Quentin. It looked like it was going to be the first Saturday in April, getting close to the tearoom's anniversary, but doable.

Getting caught up took me all morning. Lunch was a sandwich with the last of the chicken salad, along with some pickles I'd made from Nat's recipe, and I ate it at the capstan table. Afterward, I went back to my desk to face the wedding venue problem.

I brought up my list of possibilities. One was *El Rancho de las Golondrinas*, a living history museum on 200 acres of valley farmland southwest of Santa Fe. It was a beautiful place, with lots of picturesque spots where a wedding could happen. It had many more facilities than Hyde Park. It was also breathtakingly expensive, and the annual Renaissance Fair would be taking place there on our wedding date.

We could change the date, but I felt like the conflict was a prohibitive sign. We didn't need such a large venue, and it was bit out of the way.

Also, I wasn't sure Julio would be happy doing the catering there. It would take a site visit to find out, which would have to be scheduled. Frowning, I decided it was a maybe, but I'd keep looking.

I heard a car pulling up out back and figured

it must be Owen. It was almost one-thirty, and he and Dale had planned to start rehearsing at two. I went downstairs and out the back door, where Owen had backed up his SUV and was lowering the tailgate. A large, black, triangularish padded case lay on the mattress: the concert harp.

"Can I help?" I asked.

"You can open the door," he said, carefully bringing the harp out of the bed and setting it upright.

I did so, and Owen lifted the harp easily, carried it in, and set it at the foot of the stairs. He then returned to the SUV for sound equipment and a four-by-six rug to define the musicians' space, with room for the harp, a folding chair, and microphones, which I helped carry. The Bluetooth speaker went behind the staircase.

"No music stands?" I asked.

"Don't need 'em. We've memorized the set."

Very professional. I watched him cable up the sound, then uncover the harp. He took a tuning hammer out of a pocket in the padded case and began checking the pitch of the strings.

"Is there anything else I can help with?" I asked. "Would you like tea?"

"Sure, thanks."

I made a pot of Irish Breakfast in the butler's pantry. By the time it was ready, Dale had arrived and was setting up his instruments.

He had a lovely frame drum—the bodhran—with Celtic designs painted on the skin. This he propped on a stand next to his microphone, making for a nice display when he wasn't playing it. He set a pretty, pierced-tin wastebasket on top of a second speaker that was aimed toward the front of the tearoom, and put his collection of tin flutes into it so that he could easily grab whatever flute he wanted. Clever notion.

I brought mugs of tea to both of them. The hall was a little chilly; no fires in the fireplaces today. Owen finished tuning, played a few chords to make sure no strings had gone out of tune again, and took a big swallow of his tea before getting comfortable in his chair.

With the armchairs from Marigold and Poppy back in their reborn alcoves, there was no longer seating in the hall. I fetched one of the capstan chairs from Marigold and set it against the wall where I could watch and listen to the rehearsal.

"You don't mind an audience, do you?" I asked.

"Not at all," Owen said. He looked at Dale. "Ready?"

Dale nodded, raising his flute. With a lift of his chin Owen signaled the upbeat, and they were off on "Brian Boru's March." Dale switched to the bodhran on the second time through, and to my relief he kept it subdued.

They ended with a flourish, and Owen immediately went into a lively reel, the sort of song that made you want to dance. Then he switched up and played a gentle ballad, the chords of the harp hanging beautifully in the air.

The customers would love this. As the music went on, Kris came down and sat on the stairs to listen. A few minutes later Julio stepped out of the short hallway that led to the pantry and kitchen, and leaned against the wall.

Thinking I should check how the music sounded in the dining parlor, I got up and fetched a chair for Julio. The volume from the little speaker was fine; I could hear the music clearly in the alcoves, but it wasn't loud enough to overpower a conversation.

Most of the set was instrumental. The occasional vocals were excellent; Dale and Owen's voices blended well, and their harmonies were sometimes surprising. Owen sang a song in Gaelic—"Sí Beag Sí Mór"—one of my favorite of Turloch O'Carolan's works. I had no idea if he pronounced the lyrics correctly but it sounded beautiful, with a lilting harmony added on the flute by Dale.

By this time, Hanh had also come out into the hall and another chair had found its way out of the parlor for her. Dale launched into a jig, the first of three, and he and Owen pushed the tempo as hard as they could, Owen's fingers flying over the strings. He finished with a percussive thump on the harp's soundboard, and got a round of applause from the listeners.

Dale glanced up at Kris, grinning, out of breath. He put his flute into the basket with the others, sipped some water from a travel mug at his feet, then looked at Owen and nodded.

Owen played a two-chord intro, and Dale sang "Danny Boy." I understood Owen's weariness of the song, but he and Dale had come up with a simple, non-schmaltzy arrangement that was perfectly lovely. Another round of applause followed its conclusion, and Owen set the harp upright.

"Break time," he announced.

I stood. "Tea!"

The others gathered by the stairs and chatted while I stepped into the pantry, filled a kettle and set it heating, and collected more mugs and the first pot of tea. Everyone had some, even Hanh, who usually drank green tea.

I brewed a second pot and we drank most of that, too, before Owen returned to his chair and leaned the harp back again. Julio disappeared into the kitchen for a couple of minutes as the second half of the set began.

More wonderfulness, a mix of traditional and contemporary Irish music. When Dale's flute opened "She Moved Through the Fair," everyone listening held still, captivated by the haunting melody. It was possibly my favorite piece in the whole set, but they were all great.

After another lively O'Carolan number, Owen pushed the harp upright and I thought they were finished, but then he turned to his microphone and sang:

> *Oh, all the money that e'er I had,*
> *I spent it in good company*
> *And all the harm that I ever did,*
> *alas it was to none but me.*

I smiled. "The Parting Glass," the best farewell song ever written. Forget "Auld Lang Syne." This was my favorite. Owen sang it *a capella* except for some light harmonies from Dale's flute. On the last lines he was alone again, and dropped the pace just a little, suggesting a hint of regret.

> *But since it falls unto my lot*
> *that I should rise and you should not*
> *I'll gently rise and softly call,*
> *goodnight and joy be with you all.*

For a hushed moment, everyone was still. Owen's eyes were closed, a slight frown on his brow. Then he relaxed and looked up with a soft smile, and we all began to clap.

"Brilliant!" Kris said, coming to the foot of the stairs. "You should play that for Ostara. You should also record it."

"'The Parting Glass'?"

"The whole set. It's an album."

"Oh, hm," Owen said. "Getting the rights to some of it might be complicated."

"I can help with that, if you want," Kris said.

Owen glanced at Dale, who shrugged. "We'll talk," he told Kris.

"It's a marvelous set, Owen," I said, standing. "It's going to make the day magical. You'll be okay doing it three times?"

"Yeah," Dale said. "There's not that much singing, so our voices should last. We've gone three hours a couple of times, rehearsing."

I became aware of a luscious smell coming from the kitchen. Looking around, I saw that Hanh and Julio were gone. They reappeared after a couple of minutes, bearing fresh soda bread and butter. I nabbed a piece of bread and ducked into the pantry to start more tea. We all stood together chatting in the hall until the bread was gone, washed down by more Irish Breakfast. The music had not only put us in a good mood, it had made us feel like a family, and like a family, we had broken bread together.

As Kris and the chefs drifted back to their work, I collected mugs and put the chairs back in the dining parlor. Owen and Dale were packing up, and I was about to head upstairs when there was a loud banging on the front door.

We all looked up. The CLOSED sign was definitely displayed in one of the lights, because it said OPEN on the side I could see. A face appeared below it, peering in.

"Shoot," I said.

It was the Bird Woman.

8

SHE'D SEEN US, SO THERE WAS NO ESCAPE. Owen glanced at me, questioning, as he coiled a cable. I sighed and walked up the hall to the accompaniment of more banging on the door. Before opening it, I put on a smile.

"Hello, Mrs. Olavssen."

"You didn't answer my messages," she accused.

"I'm so sorry—it's been rather busy."

She opened her mouth to say more, but stopped suddenly, staring past me toward Owen. "Is that a harp?"

"Um, yes. We've just had a rehearsal for St. Patrick's Day."

"Oh, hey, cool! Can I look at it?"

Giving up, I opened the door wider to let her in. Maybe the harp would distract her from bugging me about Silly Samba.

She marched down the hall to where Owen was working. He looked up at her with polite curiosity. Dale was nowhere in sight.

"That's a concert harp," the Bird Woman informed Owen.

A smile tugged at the corner of his mouth. "Yes, it is."

"You play in the orchestra?"

"No, not since school." He tilted his head. "Have we met? At the Opera, perhaps?"

"Yeah, I go every year. You probably seen me in the club house." She was absorbed in the harp, and reached out to touch the baroque ornamentation on the pillar. Owen smiled indulgently.

She turned to me suddenly. "You got to come look at Solly Samba. It's perfect for your wedding."

Drat. "Well—"

"Sol y Sombra?" Owen said, suddenly intent.

The Bird Woman glanced at him. "Yeah."

"I thought it was privately owned."

"Yeah, but it's about to go on the market. I know the gal who's going to list it." She turned to me. "She'll let you come look, but we gotta do it before it sells, in case the buyer won't let us in."

Owen's eyes widened. *"Sol y Sombra* is for sale?"

"Yeah, gonna be," the Bird Woman said.

Owen looked at me. "We must go!"

"Uh…" I was confused, still rearranging Silly Samba into, apparently, something else in my brain. "What is *Sol y Sombra?*"

It meant "sun and shade," I knew. Owen smiled, eyes gleeful. "You'll like it!"

"It's a place for your wedding," the Bird Woman said to me. "Wanna go look now? The gal's over there and said we could come, so I came to get you."

"May I join you?" Owen said.

She looked at him. "Sure! More the merrier!"

They both turned to me expectantly. I swallowed. "Okay, sure."

I trusted Owen. If he said I needed to look at *Sol y Sombra*, I would go.

He hastily covered his harp with its padded case and set it safely against the wall, then we all piled into the Bird Woman's Cadillac, which was old—possibly vintage—but well cared-for. She turned east on Marcy Street, then south, and drove up Old Santa Fe Trail. Since she was by no means a hesitant driver, I kept my mouth shut so as not to distract her. Glancing at Owen, who had taken the back seat, I saw him intent on his phone.

The Bird Woman wound her way up into the foothills on smaller and smaller roads. Traffic was light, here, and she started chatting.

"Been to a couple of parties here," she said. "It's a really swell place. When you said you wanted your wedding outdoors, I thought about it, so I started checking. That's how I found out it was gonna be for sale."

A big, private house, I thought. Possibly with a nice yard. But how could we talk the new owner into letting us have a wedding there? It sounded unlikely, unless the Bird Woman had leverage. Maybe if the new owners didn't plan to move in right away....

No, very unlikely that it would work, but I resigned myself to looking. It wouldn't hurt, and might be fun. And at least it wasn't a disco parlor.

When we passed through a large, cast iron gate, I found myself rearranging my ideas again. Beyond the gate was a long driveway, at the end of which was a sizable parking lot. This was not just a house, although there was a very large, multi-storied adobe house before us. There were also other buildings, I saw as we got out of the car.

"This is the estate where Georgia O'Keeffe spent her last years," Owen said softly, joining me. He grinned at my astonished look. "Thought you'd like that."

A middle-aged woman in a linen pantsuit and

immaculately styled frosted hair came forward to greet us, shaking hands with the Bird Woman, who introduced us. "This here's Vickie. Vickie this is Ellen Rosings, she owns the Wisteria Tearoom. And this is…"

"Owen Hughes," Owen said, accepting the hand Vickie offered with a slight bow. "Pleased to meet you."

"Ellen here's looking for a place to get married," the Bird Woman said.

"Oh," Vickie said, glancing at Owen.

"Not to me," he said hastily. "We're just neighbors."

Vickie smiled, looking back at me. "Well, *Sol y Sombra* is a lovely place for weddings. There have been many here."

For the next hour, she led us over the twenty-acre estate, showing us the gardens, the lodge (far more elegant than Hyde Park Lodge), the meeting center, guest lodging, a theater, a huge, amazing greenhouse, and more. There was no way I could afford to rent this place for the wedding, even if it was possible, which I doubted. The fee would make *Las Golondrinas* look cheap, I was sure. So I gave up and just enjoyed the tour.

"This Bodhi tree is said to have been planted from a seed of the tree where the Buddha sat for enlightenment," Vickie told us as we stood in the greenhouse.

Owen reached out to touch the tree, enchanted. I felt as if I had stepped into a fairy tale. I was certainly out of my depth, I knew.

When we walked out onto the west-facing lawn, with a view across Santa Fe clear to the horizon and the Jemez Mountains to the northwest, I felt a pang. This would be perfect for the wedding. A beautiful garden, away from the bustle of Santa Fe, yet still in the city. There was a café kitchen adjacent to the greenhouse that would be ideal for catering an event.

It was absolutely perfect in every way, and I didn't stand a chance of getting it.

Ah, well. At least I'd been able to see it. I pictured O'Keeffe relaxing here on the lawn, watching the sunset on the horizon, and I felt something fall into place in my heart.

This was what I loved about Santa Fe, and also about O'Keeffe's artwork. Vast skies and hundred-mile vistas. Clear air and amazing sunlight. New Mexico magic at its best.

Turning, I saw the Bird Woman sitting on one of the round wooden benches encircling grand old cottonwoods that shaded the lawn—or would, when they had leafed out. Sun and shade. Yes.

A little distance beyond, Owen stood chatting with Vickie. She nodded and handed him a business card, and my heart stood still.

Oh, no.

I could *not* let Owen spend money on my wedding. He'd done too much for me already. I started toward them.

The Bird Woman stood as I came near. "Well, hope you like it!" she said, dusting off her skirt.

"It's wonderful," I said, keeping an eye on Owen and Vickie. "You're right, it would be perfect, but I—"

"Don't worry, we can make it happen," she said, with a smile that crinkled up her face. Her eyes had the same delighted gleam that Owen's had when he was about to do something outrageously generous. "I got connections."

I had to laugh, having no words. We joined Owen and Vickie, who walked with us back to the parking lot, where we all shook hands.

"We'll be in touch," the Bird Woman said to Vickie.

Vickie smiled, looking from her to me to Owen. "It's been a pleasure meeting you."

"Thank you for the tour," I said. "The estate is amazing."

We left, and I sat thinking over what I'd just seen, treasuring up the memories, as the Bird Woman drove back to the tearoom. She and Owen chatted enthusiastically about what they liked best about the estate.

Yes, they were up to mischief—they planned to finesse the use of *Sol y Sombra* for my wedding—and I'd have to be strong to resist. When the Bird Woman dropped us off and Owen and I walked up the path to the tearoom together, I paused outside the front door.

"Owen—"

"It's the perfect place, don't you agree?"

"Yes, but I can't let you spend any more money on me," I said. "It isn't right."

He looked at me with amusement. "My dear Ellen, you mistake me. Never forget that at heart, I am selfish. If I spend money on *Sol y Sombra*, it will be for my own benefit."

I gave him a skeptical look. "Renting an estate for someone else's wedding benefits you how?"

"Who said anything about renting?"

He smiled, then opened the door and headed for the foot of the stairs. Stunned, I followed him.

"You can't be serious. That estate is worth millions!"

He unplugged a microphone and put it in its case. "I think I can talk them down to twenty."

"Twenty *million dollars!?*"

"My portfolio is stock-heavy. Real estate's a great way to balance it."

"*Owen!*" I stood gaping.

He shot me a grin. "I can't let that Bodhi tree slip through my fingers. I must have it."

Dismay filled me. With that estate for inspiration, Julio could paint to his heart's content. Was I about to lose my chef?

I swallowed. "Would you live there?" I asked in a small voice.

"Oh, no," Owen said. "Perhaps later, but it's much too big, and I'm comfortable where I am. But wouldn't it be wonderful for events? Kris can have her black-and-white ball at last!"

It wasn't just me he was thinking of. The Goth community, his family, would benefit from this as well. And who knew who else? Like the Bird Woman, he would use his prosperity to uplift others.

Humbled, I watched him finish packing up his sound gear, and silently helped him carry it to the SUV. He went back for the harp, placed it tenderly on the mattress, then closed the tailgate and turned to me.

"I have to thank you, Ellen. I wouldn't have known *Sol y Sombra* was available if I hadn't met your friend. Mrs.—Olsen?"

"Olavssen."

He grinned. "She's a hoot."

"Yes, she is."

"See you Thursday." He caught me in a quick hug, then climbed into the SUV and drove away.

I watched him out of sight, still stunned.

At last I turned and went inside, thinking over the tour, realizing that Owen was not going to let me say no. Even if I refused to have the wedding there, he would buy *Sol y Sombra*. What had I done?

It would be insane to refuse, of course. The estate was exactly what I'd been looking for.

Tony would be furious. Or maybe not, but he'd definitely be uncomfortable. I had no idea what to say to him. Maybe Owen could convince him it was okay—he'd certainly backed me into a corner.

Julio and Hanh were gone. I locked the doors and went upstairs, where Kris was on the phone. With a cup of tea from the pot on the samovar, I went to the front windows and sat thinking about *Sol y Sombra*, gazing out at my far less spectacular westward view, which I still loved. I drank my tea, then went into my office, returning to reality from the dream-realm which, amazingly, looked like it was about to come true.

A text from Gina, nudging about the wedding venue. I texted back.

> Don't worry. I think I've
> got it.

It rained on St. Patrick's Day, and nobody minded. Ireland was rainy, after all, and fires in the fireplaces made the tearoom cozy. With an abundance of delightful food, and Owen and Dale's music filling the house, customers and staff alike were happy.

Nicholas had gotten permission to skip class that day and was filling in for Dale, looking charming in a pale green brocade vest and matching bow tie. A few times I caught him in the hall, entranced by the music, until he noticed me watching and ducked into the butler's pantry.

I found numerous important reasons to be downstairs that morning. Between the first and second seatings, I shared a lunch of the tea menu with Owen, Dale, Julio, and Kris at the capstan table upstairs, and we talked and laughed until we had to scurry to get ready for the next seating.

By the third seating I gave up all pretense of working and just lingered downstairs, enjoying the music all over again, not tired of any of it. I spent most of my time in the gift shop with Angela, who had come in to help after her classes. She was all smiles.

When it got busy I helped out with drop-in shoppers (we sold a lot of takeout cream tea to people who were disappointed that they couldn't be seated), and at the break I went around to each of the alcoves to say hello to the guests.

The Bird Woman had taken over the dining parlor, and once again brought guests from Esperanza Shelter. When I looked in I found that the dividing screens had been removed and all the furniture turned to face the center of the room. Dale and Owen happened to be playing a jig, and the Bird Woman—in a neon-green pantsuit—was dancing in the middle of the room with one of her guests, a plump woman who giggled constantly.

They were all wearing green leprechaun hats, and I spotted little glitter-covered pots of gold on the tables and floor and the laps of some of the guests. I wondered what treasures the Bird Woman had hidden in them, beneath what looked like gold-wrapped chocolate coins, but decided that was best left a mystery.

Everyone loved the music. Many guests asked when we would have it again, and some even asked if there would be another day of the St. Patrick's music. They wanted more.

I assured them there would be music in the future, but stopped short of promising it for the tearoom's anniversary. I'd have to start putting that together immediately.

When Owen sang "The Parting Glass" for the

final time, Angela and I stepped out into the hall to listen. Nicholas was there, too, and when he spotted me I smiled and gestured for him to stay.

Though some of the customers had finished their afternoon tea, none had left. A few came out to the hall, and when the song was done, they applauded. More customers emerged from the parlors to join them, including the Bird Woman and her guests, and the applause grew while Owen and Dale stood smiling, and finally taking a bow together.

The party was over. Guests donned their coats, chatting happily as they prepared to leave, many of them going over to thank Owen and Dale. Mrs. Olavssen's voice rose above the babble, expressing her delight, and I saw her presenting Owen and Dale with pots of gold. I smiled as Angela and I returned to the gift shop to handle the final flow of customers shopping on their way out.

The leprechaun hats paraded by on their way to the vans waiting at the curb. The rain had stopped, and the sun threw glories through the clouds as it set, shining golden through the lights around the door and spilling down the hall. Gradually, the tearoom fell quiet.

Servers cleared tables, carrying trays of china to the kitchen. The last lingering customers departed, and I locked the front door and turned the sign to CLOSED. Another day at the tearoom was over. A very good day.

Kris came downstairs, wearing her coat and bearing a fat bank bag to take to the night drop. She stood chatting with Owen and Dale as they packed up. I joined them, and Dale gave me a weary smile.

"You must be exhausted," I said. "I can't thank you both enough."

"We loved it," he said, glancing at Owen.

"Yes." Owen's smile was happy and tired. "It's been great fun. Thank you, Ellen."

"Thank *you*," I said, and gave them each an envelope containing a note, a check, and a gift card for Ten Thousand Waves. "You made magic here today."

Owen smiled. "Ah, but it wouldn't have happened if not for you. You made magic first, creating this." He gestured, sweeping his arm to encompass the tearoom, and I felt myself blush.

Nicholas and Rosa were putting on their coats. I thanked Nicholas for taking the time off from school, said goodnight to them both, and looked in on the kitchen where Dee was helping Mick with the dishes. The chefs had already gone home, and Kris waved as she went out the back door.

All well in the tearoom. I went upstairs, and realized I was on autopilot when I started to step into Kris's office instead of my own. She had shut down the samovar. All I had left to do was fetch my purse and lock my office. As I turned off the lights and started down the stairs, a lilting voice reached me from the hall below.

Good night and joy be with you all.

Nat's Fridge Pickles

Ingredients:

quart jar with lid
English cucumbers (or your favorite kind)
3 teaspoons salt
1-3 teaspoons dried dill weed (more if fresh)
1 teaspoon yellow mustard seed (optional)
1/2 cup white vinegar
2 tablespoons water (or more)

Slice cucumbers thinly (1/8-1/4 inch) and fill the jar with them. One English cucumber usually fills a jar; smaller varieties will need more cucumbers. Add the rest of the ingredients, close the lid tightly, and shake.

Put the jar in the fridge and shake it again whenever you open the door. Pickles can be eaten after a couple of hours, but will be best after several hours. Make them in the morning and they'll be ready for lunch!

Try it this way, then next time experiment with flavorings if you like. If you want the pickles a little less sour, add more water. They should keep for two or three weeks, but they probably won't be around that long!

About the Author

photo by Chris Krohn

PATRICE GREENWOOD was born and raised in New Mexico, and remembers when the Santa Fe Plaza was home to more dusty dogs than trendy art galleries. She has been writing fiction longer than she cares to admit, perpetrating over twenty published novels in various genres. She uses a different name for each genre, thus enabling her to pretend she is a Secret Agent.

She loves afternoon tea, old buildings, gourmet tailgating at the opera, ghost stories, costumes, and solving puzzles. Her popular Wisteria Tearoom Mysteries are colored by many of these interests. She is presently collapsed on her chaise longue, sipping Wisteria White tea and planning the next book in the series.